"Miss Estralita, I ain't in the travel business and, to tell you the truth, you might be safer alone than anywheres near me. Someone on the Ogallala Trail's picked up a bad habit of gunning federal deputies, of which I'm one."

She swallowed a brave little sob. "I have to get there. It's most important that I do. There's money in it for you."

"I don't charge nobody for my services except the Justice Department. Suppose you tell me what's so important," Longarm said.

"I can't. It is a secret. But I will do anything, and I mean anything, to get there..."

→ TABOR EVANS ←

ON THE
OGALLALA TRAIL

A JOVE BOOK

LONGARM ON THE OGALLALA TRAIL

A Jove Book/published by arrangement with
the author

PRINTING HISTORY
Jove edition/October 1984

ISBN: 0-515-06271-5

Chapter 1

It was raining the day they buried Pronto Malone. So everybody but the corpse in the government-issue casket was getting wetter by the minute as the minister droned on about what a swell gent the murdered federal deputy had been.

Near the foot of the open grave, Longarm was getting wetter than most. He didn't own an umbrella and hadn't deemed it proper to attend a funeral in his canary-yellow slicker. So there was nothing he could do about the rain but cuss it, silently, along with the windy minister and the shot-up cuss they were wasting all this infernal respect on.

Longarm suspected the preacher hadn't known the late Pronto Malone as well as the rest of those assembled at graveside this afternoon. For, though he obviously loved the sound of his own voice, the preaching man didn't *look* like a born liar.

Longarm shifted his weight to let the rainwater run down the left side of his tobacco-brown tweed suit for a change. He looked around casually to see if anyone else there might

1

be fighting the giggles as they had to listen polite to such whoppers about their old pard.

He couldn't catch anyone laughing openly, but more than one of his fellow deputies had to look away suddenly as their eyes met. He spied their boss, U. S. Marshal Billy Vail, standing on the far side under a big black umbrella. This time Longarm looked away as their eyes met, for he knew how rude it would have seemed to burst out laughing like a jackass with Pronto's poor little widow woman smack between them, seated under another umbrella near the long-winded minister.

Her name was Dotty, Longarm recalled. She looked sort of like a wet little sparrow bird dressed in a fresh-bought but now soggy black veil and widow's weeds. He couldn't remember if she was pretty or not and it was hard to fathom what a gal might be thinking with her face hidden under that veil. She was the only woman present, of course. It wouldn't have been seemly for the fancy gals and barmaids of Denver to attend old Pronto's burial, as good a customer as they might have found him in life, and, naturally, none of the married gents who'd worked with Pronto and had to bury an old pard right had seen fit to bring any respectable woman to the last rites of such a notorious skirt-chasing rascal.

Longarm wondered if the one gal there noticed it was an otherwise all-male crowd, or if she cared. In life, old Pronto had often boasted he was too slick to be caught by any fool wife. But unless Dotty was dumber that any human being had any right to be, she must have wondered some about the amazing amount of overtime her late husband had put in for the Justice Department without getting paid for it.

The preacher finally ran out of white lies about the man they'd all come out to bury and when Longarm saw the widow toss a spoonful of damp sand in the grave he figured it was safe to start edging back. He'd had to come. Pronto had been a fellow deputy. But Longarm was damned if he'd be a total hypocrite with that silver scoop. That last part was for friends and relations, damn it, and he'd been neither to the late Pronto Malone. He'd never even *liked* the son of a bitch.

As he headed for the livery horse he'd tethered to the graveyard fence, he heard his name called by a familiar voice and turned to see Marshal Vail bearing down on him, seated under the canopy of a hired surrey. "Tie that soggy pony to the ass end of this rig and I'll carry you back to town dry, old son," Vail said.

Longarm did as he was told. But as he climbed up beside his older, shorter, and fatter boss, he said, "It's too late to ride anywhere *dry*, Billy. But I thank you just the same for keeping me from getting even wetter. I'm sure glad you don't hold with scattering dust on the coffins of all your employees."

Vail snorted in disgust. "I showed up, didn't I? By the way, I didn't see you at the church services earlier."

Longarm said, "That's because I wasn't there. Had my train from Leadville been just a mite later I'd have had an excuse to miss the whole exercise in futility. Read about the shooting in the Union Depot and figured I'd best show. The poor cuss didn't have many friends."

Vail drove out the gateway onto the gravel road back to town. "Malone didn't have *any* friends, thanks to his big mouth and womanizing ways," he said with a grimace. "But he's dead and buried, so let's talk about more important matters. Did you get that rascal I sent you to get up Leadville way, Longarm?"

"Wouldn't have come back to Denver if I was still looking for him," Longarm said. "The case of Crazy Bob Calhoun is closed, boss."

3

Vail nodded approvingly but observed, "Won't be closed entire till the judge and jury sees fit to hang the bushwhacking bastard. Where'd you leave your prisoner, the federal lockup?"

Longarm fished out a soggy cheroot and lit it with a soggy but waterproof match on the second try. "Nope. Denver morgue. I did point out the considerable advantages of coming back with me quiet. But, well, I reckon they had good reason for calling him Crazy Bob."

"What happened, Longarm, did he draw on you?"

"Tried to. I see someone had better luck slapping leather with old Pronto Malone back there, Billy. Could you fill me in on that, some? All it said in the *Post* was that they'd shipped his remains back from Stateline, Kansas after he'd been gunned down by a person or persons unknown. I don't even know where in thunder Stateline, Kansas might be. Never heard of the place."

Vail clucked their harness roan into a trot as he replied, "That's 'cause it just happened. Stateline's a mushroom trail town over on the Ogallala Trail."

Longarm frowned thoughtfully. "This just ain't my day, I reckon," he said. "For I know where Ogallala is, if we're discussing a cow town up Nebraska way. But I'll be switched if I ever heard of any Ogallala *Trail*."

Vail nodded and said, "*That* just happened, too. You know how proddy settlers can get when they see cows cutting across their south forty. So most of the old market trails like the Goodnight and such have been twisted all out of shape or even closed entire. This year, Washington declared a new trail open to the drovers. It runs from the Texas Panhandle, across No Man's Land, west of the Indian Nation, and follows the Kansas–Colorado line up to Ogallala, Nebraska, where the critters can be poked aboard the U.P. for train rides to Omaha, Chicago, and such."

Longarm took a drag on his cheroot as he drew the new line on his mental map. Then he said, "Makes sense. Since the land office don't allow a homestead claim to straddle a state or territorial line, there might be a way to wedge a cow between fences along that route. I know about mushroom towns. Whores and gamblers don't work much under wide-open prairie sky and most cowhands would rather belly up to a bar under at least a canvas roof after a long day in the saddle. What was the late Pronto Malone doing in such an unseemly neighborhood—aside from getting shot, I mean?"

"He was in Stateline 'cause that's where I sent him, of course," Vail said. "You remember the Richardson brothers, Tex and Reb?"

Longarm nodded. "Yep. Locked horns with 'em a couple of times in the past, without serious consequences. They do have a habit of branding lots of Texas beef as the property of their own Rocking X. But, so far, they've never been dumb enough to do anything federal."

"You're speaking of the good old days, before the price of beef rose so high," Vail said. "I sent Pronto over to discuss some Indian beef stolen from the Osage herd. Two Osage cowhands and a white Indian agent managed to get killed trying to prevent the purloinment, making the whole operation federal as hell!"

Longarm stared thoughtfully at his boss for a time before he said, "Well, you sure look sober this afternoon, Billy. But what were you drinking the day you sent poor old Pronto Malone to arrest a hardcased cuss like Tex Richardson? I mean, I never had much use for Pronto, neither, but..."

"Back off and show some respect for your elders, damn it," snapped Vail. "I never sent Malone to arrest Tex Richardson. Old Tex is down at the Rocking X home spread at the moment. Likely coveting his neighbor's wife and other

5

livestock. We got a tip the older brother, Reb, was leading the trail herd this time."

"Billy, nobody riding for the Rocking X is all that civilized!"

"Damn it, Longarm, I never sent Malone to *arrest* either brother. I wouldn't send *you* to shoot it out with the whole damned Rocking X and we both know you can't arrest a trail boss without the informed consent of his considerable employees. I sent Malone over to Stateline undercover. His job was to just sit there spitting and whittling till the Rocking X market herd come through. We still don't know for certain it was the Richardsons as stole and murdered in the Osage Strip. They're just sort of high on our list of suspicions."

Longarm looked away without comment. Vail snapped, "Wipe that smug, disgusted look off your face. That's an order. Pronto's orders weren't to get his fool self killed. He was supposed to do no more than take a casual interest in passing cows and wire me the minute he spied one with a suspicious or even recent-looking brand. Any arresting as had to be done was to be done further north by a posse of deputies loaded for bear."

Longarm still looked disgusted as he said, "I already had that part figured, Billy. Let's study more on how he wound up dead. Does anyone have any educated notion where the Rocking X herd might be right now?"

"They ain't passed through Stateside yet. I'd know, for I sent Deputy Flynn over there the moment the local marshal wired us about Pronto. I'd say that lets the Richardson brothers off, on Pronto's murder, at least."

Longarm shrugged. "Maybe. Unless Pronto was gunned by a scout or more they sent ahead. How much do we really know about Pronto's last shootout? The *Post* didn't have a lot to say about it."

Vail sighed. "That's likely 'cause the details are sort of

6

fuzzy, old son. No witnesses have come forward who saw the beginning of the fight. But when guns started going off out front of the Last Chance Saloon, a lot of heads naturally wound up turning. Pronto was already on the ground, under a cloud of shotgun smoke. So nobody could offer a good describing of the hazy figure ducking between the buildings with a smoking scattergun at port arms. The local coroner is a dentist who might or might not know anything about medicine. But his opinion that the cause of death was two charges of twelve-gauge number nine buck, fired at point-blank range, seems a sensible assumption to me. I had to identify the body when they shipped it back to Denver and, Jesus, what a mess!"

Longarm smoked silently as they swung a corner to drive west on paving under an arcade of cottonwood shade trees. There was nothing on the rain-wet sandstone walks to distract him as he painted pictures in his head. Then he shook his head and said, "Somebody's left something out, Billy. Pronto had his faults, but we never called him Pronto because he was *slow*."

Vail nodded. "I know. I'd have fired him long ago, had he not been a pretty good lawman, when you could get him to stop sniffing at skirts. I've been pondering that shootout, too. It does seem odd a person or persons unknown could walk up to old Pronto in broad daylight, carrying a twelve-gauge shotgun, without old Pronto *noticing*."

Longarm nodded back and said, "Pronto was better with a gun than he seemed to think he was with women. I've seen him strike out with more than one pretty ankle in the past. But I never saw anyone beat old Pronto to the draw in what's starting to sound like a fair fight."

"Hell, if you'd ever seen him lose a gunfight in the past, we wouldn't be talking about the one he just lost," Vail said. "Like the song says, there's never a pony that couldn't

7

be rode, and there's never a rider that couldn't be throwed. Old Pronto just run into someone even faster, is all."

Longarm shook his head. "I can't picture it happening the way everyone says it did, Billy. I can see a quick-draw artist beating anyone on an off day. But Pronto was one sudden gunslick, on the job and on the prod. So how in thunder could a total stranger just walk up to him with a loaded shotgun and blow him away without him even trying to fight back?"

Vail said, "Maybe it wasn't a total stranger and maybe he *did* try to fight back. Like I said, nobody saw the beginning of the fight."

"Pronto and me had a wagering contest out to the pistol range one afternoon, Billy," Longarm said. "We come out about even, and I wound up sort of thankful that the son of a bitch was on my side. When old Pronto decided to draw his sidearm, said sidearm got drawed . . . well, *pronto!* So if he died with his gun still holstered, he died without any suspicion at all of the other's intent."

Longarm took another drag on his cheroot and added, "That takes us back to what you said about the killer maybe not being a total stranger to him, Billy. I reckon you or me could have walked up to old Pronto hefting a scattergun. But a stranger won't work. Pronto wouldn't have trusted a strange *lady* approaching him with a shotgun in the open, and Pronto trusted ladies more than I do."

They came to a cross street. Vail reined in at the corner and took out his pocket watch before he said, "Well, the day's too shot to go back to the office, now. You want to come by my place for supper with me and the wife, Longarm?"

Longarm shook his head. "You go on home, Billy. The rain can't wet me more than I already am and Henry might not have closed the office yet."

Vail frowned. "If he locks up before six I'll fire him. But what in the hell do *you* have to do at the office so late, Longarm?"

The tall, dripping deputy said, "I'm going to need travel vouchers and such, ain't I?"

Vail looked blank and asked, "Travel vouchers to where and what for? I ain't got another case in mind for you at the moment, old son."

Longarm said, "Sure you do. Someone has to go after the killer of Pronto Malone, right?"

"Wrong. I already told you I sent Flynn over to the Ogallala Trail, damn it!"

"Now don't get your bowels in an uproar, Billy. I won't steal Flynn's brand inspecting from him. I just have to nail Malone's killer."

Vail raised an eyebrow. *"Have* to, Longarm? I didn't know you was so fond of the late Pronto Malone."

Longarm swung down from the surrey and looked back up at Vail with a sort of puzzled expression of his own as he replied, "To call a spade a spade, I disliked him intense, and I suspicion not even his pretty widow woman will really miss the son of a bitch."

"I suspicion you're right, Longarm. So tell me why it's so important to you to avenge the poor bastard not even a wife has reason to miss?"

Longarm shrugged. "Ain't sure," he said. "Maybe it's because the poor bastard was wearing the same badge I carry when he was murdered. Don't *matter* how I might or might not have felt about old Pronto. Killing a deputy U. S. marshal *can't* be constitutional!"

Chapter 2

By the time the prissy clerk at the Denver federal building had typed up all the fool papers he'd need in triplicate, there was no way in hell Longarm could catch the evening east-bound combination. So, looking on the bright side, he rode through the rain back up to Sherman Avenue in search of consolation regarding the most unfortunate timetable.

The widow woman he'd last seen out at the graveyard in this same damned rain might or might not have had a pretty face under that black veil. But the widow woman who lived on Sherman Avenue was pretty for certain and built more spectacular. She'd also been a widow woman a lot longer and she and Longarm had a sort of understanding.

At least, he'd thought they had, until she opened the door of her fancy brownstone house to see him dripping all over her doormat and said, "You, you uncouth cowboy! Didn't I tell you never to darken my door again, you brute?"

Longarm grinned down at her, admiring the view down the front of her half-open silk kimono. "I do recall you

10

saying something to that effect as I was leaving the other morn, little darling. But, to tell the truth, your exact words were drowned out by all the crockery you was throwing at the door as I closed it, discreet."

She tried not to laugh as she insisted, "I meant what I said, you bastard. Go away. You're dripping all over everything and if you came all this way in the rain to say you're sorry—"

"I just missed a train," Longarm cut in. "There's another one leaving at four in the morning. So if I mean to be aboard her it means I got to get out of here by no later than three-thirty."

She sighed. "Oh, hell, I'd planned such a swell argument. But if we have less than ten hours for . . . well . . . reconciliation, we'd best get cracking."

"I was hoping I'd been forgiven," he said. "I have to put my hired mount under a roof first. Is your back door open, little darling?"

"It will be. Hurry, you brute."

He did, but it still took some time to rub the wet hide of the unsaddled livery mount more or less dry with sacking. By the time he got back to the house he was sure he was at least as anxious as the widow woman to kiss and make up.

He was wrong. When he locked the back door after him in the dark kitchen and moved out into the hall, the widow woman was not to be seen. So he called out, "Hey, little darling, where are you?" and her voice floated down the stairs, sort of throaty, to reply, "Up here, of course, and if you don't get up here this instant I mean to start without you!"

He entered the widow woman's bedroom to find his current port in the storm already in bed, in a mighty saucy position. Her kimono now hung over a chair in the corner

11

and her Junoesque bare rump had two pillows under it, offering a mighty interesting view of the Grand Canyon and Twin Peaks beyond the rolling pink prairies of her hourglass torso. She said, "Oh, Lord, you're still dripping, poor baby. Get out of those wet duds and dry yourself off with that towel over the foot of the bed."

He did as he was told and the widow woman giggled at his goose bumps as he rubbed his clammy hide down with the cloth. He chuckled back at her and tossed the towel aside to join her. But as he took her in his arms she gasped. "Jesus, you're cold and wet as a frog's belly!"

He said, "I noticed. I could leap in a hot tub down the hall, if you've a fire going in your heater downstairs."

She wrapped her plump arms around him and drew him closer as she protested with a shiver, "Don't you dare. You're not that cold, and I've got all the fire you need right here betwixt my thighs. I've always wondered what the princess saw in that frog, anyway."

But when he rolled into her friendly saddle of thigh flesh and parted her welcome mat with his rain-soaked tool she gasped. "Help, I'm being raped by an icicle!"

He said it felt to him as if he'd just poked it in a furnace. But in no time at all they both agreed the temperature was just delightful. So after they'd shared an orgasm old-fashioned she said, "That was a mighty interesting first course. Now that you're forgiven, let's get down to some good old dirty screwing!"

He laughed. "Hold on a minute, little darling. I told you I had to light out no later than three-thirty. So we'd best set the alarm lest I fall asleep in your loving arms."

She agreed and slid out from under him to fetch the big brass alarm clock from her dresser across the room. He stared at her considerable curves as she stood naked on the rug, resetting the clock. "I'd best hang up your duds while

12

I'm out from under you," she said. "They'll mildew for sure, piled up in such a wet wad."

She looked even more interesting in the buff as she moved about near the foot of the bed, bending from time to time to pick up another wet garment. By the time she got back in bed with him Longarm had recovered his wind and his erection had thawed out just fine. But a lawman had to keep his mind on his duties to the taxpayers, so he asked her if she'd set the clock. She dimpled down at him and said, "Don't worry, dear. I set it for midnight. You'll have plenty of time to make your train, you mean old thing."

He frowned. "Midnight's sort of early to wake up for a four-in-the-morning train, ain't it?"

She frowned back at him and asked, "Don't you mean to kiss me goodbye proper, you brute?"

He laughed and started to haul her down beside him. "No, we'd better save your strength for later," she said. "Let me get on top this time."

He did, and there was a lot to be said for reclining at ease while she had her wicked way with him. As she got to bouncing her hourglass figure up and down her big creamy breasts got to bobbing alarmingly. He reached up to cup one in each palm and she hissed, "Yes! Tickle my nipples, Custis."

He'd already started rolling them between his thumbs and fingers by the time she'd finished asking. One of the nice things about making love to an old pard was that a man knew how from the start. Longarm had long since discovered that no two women were exactly alike in bed, bless their sweet hides, and more than once duty had called him away just as he was getting to know a passing fancy's favorite pleasures. He knew he was treating this one right when she moaned in growing pleasure and leaned forward to shove her aroused left nipple in his face. He'd no sooner

13

started sucking her left nipple good than she exploded in orgasm on his shaft.

He wasn't there himself, yet, so he rolled her over and under as she protested, "Wait. I'm too sensitized to keep going, dear. Let me get my breath back, for God's sake!" But he knew her of old and knew better than to pay attention as he pounded hard in her quivering love box until she came again with him.

As they went limp in one another's arms the widow woman marveled, "That was lovely, Custis. I was so afraid you wouldn't be your old self tonight. I mean, I know how sneaky you are with the other women in your life, you brute."

Longarm didn't answer. He didn't want her throwing any more of her store-bought china at his fool head and he knew she might if they got on that subject again.

One of the only things he didn't like about the widow woman was that she talked dirty, once she'd come a couple of times. He'd explained the first night they'd met, even before he'd made love to her, that a man who packed a badge and lived by the gun had no right to settle serious with one gal. She'd said she understood. But after they'd become good pals her feminine notions had surfaced and, every once in a while, she got to talking spiteful about his time in the field. She even said that when he was out on a case she was true to him. His mild observation that if she was she was mighty dumb had resulted in more screaming and flying crockery than he was prepared for tonight, so he thought he'd best change the subject fast.

He started moving in her again. "Not so soon, dear," she said. "I want to make it last. Can't we just sort of cuddle and talk a spell?"

Talking could be dangerous with this particular gal, since the widow woman wasn't just handsome and sexy. She had

14

a mighty sharp mind as well. It stood to reason a young widow woman with the estate of a rich husband to manage had to have her wits about her. She'd told Longarm, earlier in the game, that she had no intention of ever marrying up again, lest she lose control of her own money. She was sneaky as well as smart.

She was thoughtful, as well, he saw, when she reached across him for the cheroots and matches she'd taken from his duds to dry out on the bed table. She placed a cheroot between his lips and lit it for him before she cuddled down with her unbound head on his shoulder and said, "Oh, this feels comfy. What shall we talk about, dear?"

"Ain't sure. You ever hear the one about the three bears?"

"I like the frog prince better. Tell me about this case you're on. It must be important if you have to get up before dawn. Or do you know some barmaid who gets off at four A.M., you animal?"

He chuckled and said he wished he did. Then he quickly added, "I got to see a killer about a killing, over on the Ogallala Trail."

Naturally she'd never heard of the spanking new cattle trail, so he had to fill her in on the case, up to showing up wet and horny on her doorstep.

The widow woman took more interest in the business of menfolk than some gals, being a businesswoman herself. She made him tell her twice about the killing of Pronto Malone and, when he had, she said, "I might have known you were involved with another woman, damn it!"

He frowned and blew a thoughtful smoke ring as he wondered what on earth had gotten into her pretty head now. "Honey, I ain't going all the way to the Kansas line to play slap and tickle with another gal. I got nice gals right here in Denver to play with."

"I'll remember that *plural*, you brute," she said. "But,

seriously, dear, isn't it an obvious case of *cherchez la femme?*"

Longarm read more than he let on, so he knew what her fancy French phrase meant, but he wasn't sure how it fit the killing of Pronto Malone. "No witness to the killing mentioned skirts on the shotgun-toting whomsoever, honey," he said.

She said, "Pooh, you just told me nobody got a good look at the killer. Can't you see it had to be a woman?"

"Not hardly," he said. "It's sort of hard to picture a gal walking down the streets of Stateline with a sun bonnet and a twelve-gauge."

The widow woman insisted, "You told me Pronto Malone was on a case and on the prod, and that he was a skilled gunfighter with a lightning draw, right?"

"Yeah, that's why they called him Pronto. And he *was* almost as famous as a skirt chaser, too. But, Jesus, a skirt with a *shotgun?*"

"Why not? I've potted more than one rabbit in my back garth with my late husband's old scattergun. I know you think it's silly. But that's my whole point. A woman can pull a trigger just as well as a man. But your skirt-chasing deputy might not have remembered that when he saw some demure young miss approaching with her daddy's shotgun in her dainty hands. If she was at all pretty, he might well have stopped her, grinning, to ask what she was hunting, and—"

"It works," Longarm cut in. "That ain't saying the killer *has* to be a woman. But I admire your notion that the killer was able to surprise old Pronto by looking at least as disharmful as a woman."

He snuffed out his cheroot and took her in his arms again, saying, "Bless your sweet hide, you've given me some mighty interesting notions."

"Good. Let's try it from behind this time. Or are we still talking about that dumb old deputy getting shotgunned?"

He laughed and said, "Both," as he helped her into a kneeling position with her ample derrière aimed over the edge of the bed and rose to the occasion in every way, bracing his bare feet on the rug as he entered her like a stallion.

She arched her back and crooned, "Oh, heavenly!" as he cupped a well-padded hip bone in either hand and proceeded to treat her right. But one of the nice things about screwing with old pards, once the first excitement simmered down, was that pals could enjoy interesting conversations, even screwing, and he knew she liked to chat.

So as he humped her at a comfortable lope he mused aloud, "I'll buy a killer in skirts when I see one. But lots of men could look harmless enough to a bragging bully like old Pronto. A skinny kid, for instance, or mayhaps a harmless-looking gent dressed like a deacon."

The widow woman started wagging her tail like a happy pup or a nervous cat as she replied in the same conversational tone, "You mark my words and watch out for a fancy gal or a schoolmarm packing a twelve-gauge, Custis. You men are all alike when it comes to pretty women. And, speaking of coming, could you move a little faster, damn it?"

Chapter 3

The eastbound combination crossed the Kansas border less than six hours out of Denver, of course, but nowhere near the new trail town of Stateline, if the new government survey map had it located right. So Longarm got a neighborly brakeman to stop the combination on what had been open prairie the last time he'd looked and let his fresh mount from the same livery down the ramp from the forward boxcar. As the train tooted its whistle and rolled on, Longarm looked about and saw he was not alone out here in the middle of what had usually been nowhere. A few hundred yards away some gents were putting up a frame building's raw pine skeleton. Beyond it, two other boxy, unpainted buildings were already up. As Longarm led his chestnut gelding along the tracks toward them the colored gents hammering two-by-fours went on working. A white man wearing blue denims and an equally functional brace of sixguns strode casually to meet him. Longarm saw he was keeping his hands polite, so he did the same until they got close

18

enough to talk. Then he said, "Morning. I'm looking for a town called Stateline. This ain't it, is it?"

The stranger spat thoughtfully and gazed past Longarm. "This here's the town of Kanorado—or it will be, once we gets it built," he said. "Stateline's a day's ride south. How come you're riding an army saddle, pilgrim?"

Longarm said, "I know a McClellan is a ball buster, for I've busted many a ball on her. But a man who rides serious has to consider his mount. I ain't cow. I'm law."

The denim-clad man looked somewhat friendlier as he answered, "I'm law, too. Name's Watson, Duke Watson. I'm the elected town marshal of Kanorado."

Longarm kept a straight face as he looked past Watson at the handful of colored workmen and decided not to question the last election in this unincorporated mushroom. Watson said, "I was afeared for a minute you was some sort of tinhorn, riding in uninvited. You got to have a license to set up shop in this town, mister, ah . . . ?"

"Oh, sorry. I'm Deputy U. S. Marshal Custis Long, out of the Denver office."

Watson whistled softly. "I've heard of you, Longarm. Don't want no *trouble* with you, neither! You just tell me who you want here in Kanorado and I'll help you catch the son of a bitch!"

Longarm smiled. "I'm happy to say I ain't after anyone in your fair city, Duke," he told the marshal. "I didn't even know it was here until I got off the train just now. But as long as we're discussing wants so friendly, could you point out this here Ogallala Trail I've heard so much about?"

Watson waved a casual hand between them and said, "We're just about smack on it, Longarm. It runs along the state line, official. Of course, since there's no sign posts, a little guesswork is involved."

Longarm stared south, since that was the direction he'd

be going. The rain the night before had matted the summer-killed shortgrass flat and cow-pat brown. But here and there he could see where a passing hoof had scalped the sod to the damp 'dobe soil. "I see it ain't been used much as yet," he said.

Watson said, "Just wait till the fall roundup's over. This is now the best and damned near only way to get southern beef to the U.P. line, and that's where the price of beef is highest this year. My pards and me figure plenty of business afore long, serving the drovers' . . . ah . . . comforts."

Longarm was too polite to ask what sort of comforts the boomers had in mind, but he couldn't help pointing at the nearby tracks and asking, "Wouldn't this be as good a place to load beef aboard a train as up north in Ogallala, Duke?"

Watson shook his head. "You looks cow and you talks cow, but you ain't been reading the market prices much, I'll vow. They got plenty of *railroads* now in *Texas*. The trick ain't getting the beef aboard a train, Longarm. The trick is getting 'em to Omaha or Chicago, where the price is highest right now!"

Longarm smiled sheepishly and said, "I'll have to allow the cattle business has gotten complicated as hell since last I rode with Captain Goodnight and such. But I ain't looking for cows. I'm sort of anxious to talk to some gents as might be driving cows, though. Could you tell me if the Rocking X herd's been by here recent?"

Watson shook his head. "That's an easy one. They ain't. I'd know if that particular outfit was in my neck of the woods, for I makes it a practice to avoid the company of the Richardson brothers. They ain't the ones you're after, I hope?"

"I hope so, too. But I still got to talk to them and if they ain't been this far north yet, they must be somewhere south."

He added it had been nice talking to Watson as he turned

to fork himself aboard the gelding. But before he could ride off, Watson said, "Hey, Longarm?" and when Longarm turned in the saddle the marshal added, "I know you know the Richardsons and the suspense involved in meeting up with 'em. But if you're heading for Stateline, watch out for an outfit calt the Double Eight. The ramrod's a harmless-looking kid calt Four Eyes. He wears specs and packs a double-action S&W."

"I'll keep the Double Eight in mind, Duke. Are they supposed to be as mean as the Richardson brothers?"

Watson spat again. "Meaner. They say when Four Eyes is in town, the Richardson brothers hide out till he leaves!"

By noon the summer sun and prairie winds had dried the grass all around as well as Longarm's tweeds. So the new trail was easier to travel, now that untrod shortgrass stems were standing up again. The grass stomped flat for keeps cut a swathe about a hundred yards wide due north and south, according to the sun. There wasn't much else to look at this far east on the high plains. It wasn't quite as flat as the Nebraska prairie. Nothing was as flat as the Nebraska prairie. So he got to ride over a gentle swell or down into a shallow draw from time to time. But it was still mighty tedious scenery, and Watson had said he had a day of it ahead of him. Hopefully less than a day if they both judged riding time the same way. He'd left Kanorado around ten. A twelve-hour ride figured to put him in Stateline around ten in the evening. He reined his mount to a slower walk as he told it, "We'd best study on this, pard. Ten P.M. ain't the best time to hit a strange cow town, you know. Midnight might be more discreet. By then most of the mean drunks should be in jail or sleeping it off and we don't want nobody but Deputy Flynn to greet us, quiet."

The gelding didn't argue. That was one of the nice things

about talking to critters. But when they topped the next rise, Longarm saw dust behind them and reined in to study on the company he might or might not want on the trail.

The buckboard raising all that dust stopped dead on another rise to the north and Longarm muttered, "Great minds must run in the same channels, horse. Let's put some distance between us and them so they can drive south some more, unworried."

He heeled the chestnut into a lope down the far side, not looking back as they topped the next rise and kept going. He'd already figured the bright colors on the buckboard seat spelled two gals, riding alone, and he knew he'd scare them even more if he kept looking back at them. But this was a hell of a way to ride into Stateside *slow*. So as he loped his mount he kept his eyes peeled for a draw deep enough to hide out in so they could pass him without getting spooked again. There had to be some good cover out here, somewhere. In the Shining Times this had been the Southern Cheyenne and Arapaho hunting ground, and more than one old cavalry trooper had learned the hard way how easy it was to hide a whole Indian village on what looked like wide-open prairie.

He kept his eyes peeled for a cottonwood or crack-willow top pretending to be a low bush as it grew a mite taller in the bottom of some watered draw. But topping yet another rise he spotted something up ahead that surprised him entirely. So he reined his mount to a walk as he rode in for a better look.

A small sod hut grew out of the prairie just inside the Colorado line. That looked reasonable enough. But the Glidden-wire fence stretched smack across the public trail made no sense at all. Had some fool nester missed his lawful homestead claim by a mile or more?

As he rode closer, Longarm saw that the fence couldn't

be enclosing any lawful quarter-section claim. For it ran miles or more east and west of the soddy. He could see now that there was a gate in the fence, smack on the trail. That made a little more sense. Maybe someone had strung a drift fence there for some reason. But the reason wasn't easy to grasp for a man who'd driven his share of cows in his day.

He saw a couple of gents coming out of the soddy as he approached the gate, so he figured he'd let them tell him what in thunder they'd strung all that wire for.

As Longarm reined in near the gate with a quizzical smile the older and meaner-looking one of the pair called out, "It's gonna cost you two bits, pilgrim."

Longarm asked politely, "Two bits for what, friend? I got water in my canteen and I just parted friendly with a lady. So would one of you be kind enough to swing that gate open for me?"

The younger one, wearing bib overalls and a Henry repeater, laughed and said, "Two bits is what it costs to ride through, pilgrim. This here's a toll gate, see?"

Longarm snorted in disbelief but kept his voice friendly as he said, "No, it ain't. This here is a U. S. government cattle trail, open to the general public, of which I am one. So why should I give anyone two bits to pass on peaceable?"

The older self-appointed toll taker shrugged. "You can pass through free on foot, I reckon. We only charges two bits a critter, which I'm sure you'll agree that chestnut is."

His junior partner added, "You can even ride around, if you've a mind to. Fence don't stretch more'n three or four miles either way. But you looks like a sensible gent. So just give us a quarter and we'll open the gate for you, hear?"

Longarm didn't answer as he added in his head. He saw they'd figured the price about right. Few riders with a lick of sense would risk a fight with two armed men for two

23

bits. A herd of cows would add up to a more serious discussion, he felt sure. But that was *their* problem. He shrugged and reached in his pocket, saying, "You boys sure must enjoy living dangerous, but it's getting too hot to fight over small change."

That might have ended it had not the younger rascal suddenly said, "Hot damn, here comes some more customers, Pop. What do we charge a buckboard, team and all?"

Longarm turned in his saddle to see the two gals he'd been trying to shed driving in from the north, unconcerned, now that they saw what looked like a calm discussion over a homestead fence. He knew they saw the gate and, like he had, expected it to be opened for them, polite.

The older squatter grinned and said, "Let's see, now. Fifty cents for the team, two bits an axle for the rig, that makes her a buck even, unless them gals would like us to take it out in trade. They looks like fancy gals to me, son."

The younger one snickered. "Hot damn, let's invite 'em in for some fun, Pop. I ain't had a woman in a coon's age!"

Longarm sighed, drew his .44, and proceeded to put the toll gate out of business.

As he'd hoped, both moronic louts were distracted by the approaching gals and hadn't noticed his slapping leather until too late—almost. He blew the older man's dim brains away with his first shot. But even as he aimed at the younger one, the Henry repeater in his hands came up to fire back, so they both got hit. But fortunately Longarm only took a round through the crown of his hat while his own round caught its victim in the teeth and kept going, making an awesome mess out of the nape of his neck.

Leaving the gals in the buckboard behind him on their own for a moment, Longarm rolled out of the saddle, gun in hand, and rolled under the bottom strand of the illegal fence to leap back to his feet and charge the house. As he did so the soddy's one door opened and the third man he'd been afraid might be inside ran out, firing wild and blind in every direction, until Longarm jackknifed him to the ground with another .44-40 slug aimed better, at his belt buckle. The big lawman kept going, leaping over the third body to fire into the gaping doorway for luck as he bored in on it. But when he bulled his way inside, with only two rounds left in his smoking sixgun, he saw it was safe to study on reloading. The interior of the soddy reeked of rotgut and sweaty blankets, but was otherwise harmlessly empty.

As he stepped back outside, thumbing fresh rounds in his sidearm, he was surprised to see the gals in the buckboard hadn't lit out as he'd expected. They were frozen on the seat of their rig, staring at him wide-eyed. He walked over to the gate, stepping over a body on the way, and unlatched it to swing it wide, calling out, "It's all right, ladies. I'm the law and, as you can see, these gents wasn't."

Neither girl said a word or moved a muscle. He holstered his .44 and took out his wallet, holding it high for the sun to glint off his silvery badge as he insisted wearily, "You can drive on through, now. What we had here was an unauthorized toll gate, run by idjets. Do you ladies live around here?"

The plump brunette holding the reins gulped. "We were on our way to the town of Stateline, sir," she said.

The thinner blonde at her side said, "She's Flo and I'm Becky. Please don't rob us, mister. We've hardly any money left, and—"

Longarm laughed and cut in, "It's just as well I got to this here unauthorized roadblock first, then. If you won't take my badge's word we'll just say no more about it. It's been nice talking to you, ladies, but I got a few chores to do here before I can ride on."

Neither answered. So he put his wallet away and turned from them to study some on what he'd just wrought.

None of the bodies had any I.D. and their dead faces rang no bells in his fair memory of wanted posters. So he pocketed the few bucks they'd been packing between them on the principal of finders, keepers. Their firearms were antiques scarcely worth packing off, but he unscrewed all the trigger assemblies and pocketed them for now, lest children or worse get in trouble playing with the old guns. He found three mistreated scrub ponies tethered behind the soddy. He turned them loose without saddle or harness to fend for themselves. From the way they ran off, he was sure they thought they could take better care of themselves than any humans had recently.

The considerable fence the saddle tramps had strung puzzled him some. He couldn't see them *buying* that much wire. On the other hand, there was many an abandoned homestead on the high plains these days, thanks to the drought of the Seventies.

When he turned back to find out if he still had his own mount, he did. The chestnut was grazing peaceably near the gate with its reins dragging. The buckboard full of womankind was still there, too. He walked over, nodded to the gals, and remounted the gelding before he said, "Well, you ladies can stay here if you like. I got to move on down the road."

Miss Flo stared wide-eyed at him. "We're scared," she said. "They told us it was wild out here, but not *this* wild! Who were those men you just shot down like dogs?"

Longarm shook his head. "I hardly ever shoot dogs, ma'am," he told her. "The rascals was armed and it was three to one. As to who they might have been, I got too much on my plate to worry about such minor details. I'll mention our business discussion to the coroner at Stateside and he can do whatever he's a mind to about their mortal remains. But I can't hardly report this mess to the coroner at Stateside before I *get* to Stateside. So that's where I'm headed."

Miss Flo stared silently at her blond traveling companion. Then she turned to Longarm to ask, "Would you be kind enough to escort us to Stateline, sir? We've neither guns nor money and, as we just saw, the country out here is wilder than we were led to believe!"

He said he'd noticed that and clucked his mount through the gate as they followed. On the far side where it was wide enough to ride beside the buckboard he did so, lighting a smoke to study some without giving his word one way or the other. Flo and Becky talked like school gals but they dressed more flashy. The plump brunette wore a low-cut red satin outfit hardly suited to travel on the high plains by any gal, and the silly little hat pinned atop her black curls didn't shade her turned-up nose worth mention. The blonde Becky wore an outfit of sky blue, now a mite dusty from travel. He glanced in the buckboard behind them and saw they didn't have much baggage. No more than a couple of carpetbags and feed sacks, with a water bag for their team. It was easy to believe they were broke, less easy to fathom what in thunder they were doing out here. He decided not to ask. It was none of his business. But as he spied what looked like a clump of soapweed on a rise over to the east he said, "I ain't eaten yet and it's well past noon. There should be water and some shade over yonder in that draw, ladies."

Naturally they both asked him what draw he was talking about. He found it easier just to lead them off across the prairie until they topped the last rise and could see for themselves. They both gasped in delight as they stared down into the tree-shaded depths where a little sandy stream ran between banks of emerald-green grass. Flo asked him how he'd known this precious dell, as she called it, was there. "Used to scout Indians for the army," he said. "You'd best put a foot against that brake handle going down, Miss Flo."

She knew how to drive, at least. In no time at all they were sitting in the grass under the cottonwood canopy as Longarm unsaddled his mount and unharnessed their team to graze freely, knowing no horse with a lick of sense was about to run off across sun-baked prairie with green grass and water free for the taking. He unlashed his saddlebags and brought them over to where the gals were seated by the stream. Flo, the boldest, had already taken off her high-buttons to soak her feet in the water. He didn't care. Her feet looked clean and he could always refill the canteens upstream.

Longarm broke out the canned tomatoes and beans he'd meant to enjoy alone on the trail, saying, "Sorry I can only offer you ladies range grub. I wasn't expecting to dine in such fancy company."

The blonde looked dubiously at the battered cans and asked how he intended to cook their noon dinner. "Don't have to cook it," he said. "That's why it's range grub."

As he took out his pocketknife to open the cans the brunette turned out a better sport as well as bolder. "I'm too hungry to worry about whether it's cooked or not," she declared. "I vow I could eat a horse right now, raw!"

She must have meant it. Longarm had thought he'd broken out enough for three normal appetites. But as the two gals went to work on the canned tomatoes and beans, swilling from the cans like cups, he saw he'd have to dig deeper in his saddlebags if he meant to eat at all himself.

He found a chunk of jerky to chew as the hungry gals wolfed down what he'd planned on lasting him to Stateline. But he'd had breakfast on the train and suspicioned they

28

hadn't had a meal worth mention in recent memory.

He took off his Stetson and leaned back in the grass, chewing jerky, as he tried to resist asking questions. Billy Vail hadn't sent him over here to question half-starved she-males and, despite the widow woman's suggestion of *cherchez la femme*, they wouldn't fit, if neither had ever been to Stateline as yet.

The saddle tramps he'd just had it out with made no more sense as the killer or killers of Pronto Malone. In the first place, they hadn't owned a twelve-gauge between them. And, in the second place, old Pronto never would have let such mean-looking gents walk up to him with a scattergun in broad daylight without at least putting a mighty thoughtful hand on his own gun grips. And once a quick-draw artist like the late Pronto Malone had his gun in hand, it was coming out of its holster, even if he had to draw it *dead*.

He gave up on the jerky and lit a cheroot for dessert. Flo asked Becky why she didn't take off her shoes and splash her feet in the water, too. The blonde said, "It does look refreshing, but do we have the time?"

Longarm nodded and said, "Sure, you can *swim* in the creek for all I care. It's the hottest time of day, up where we just come from, and I'd like to time it so's we get to Stateline around midnight."

"Why so late?" asked Flo as Becky shyly commenced unbuttoning her shoes, exposing her stockings and a little more. Longarm looked away politely, and explained, "I'm meeting another deputy at the one hotel in town. You ladies can likely find a bug-free bed there as well. But we don't want a strange rider and two pretty gals causing comment on the main drag if a herd's in town. Most of the dust and busted glass should have settled down by midnight, though."

Becky stopped what she was doing and sobbed, "Flo, I want to go home!"

But Flo was made of sterner stuff, even though she was built softer. She said, "We can't go home now, you ninny. There's no home to go home to. Don't you remember all the names those old biddies back in Iowa called us as they frog-marched us out of town?"

"Maybe they've forgotten by now," the blonde suggested hopefully.

"Oh, shut up and put your feet in the water," her friend said.

So Becky did, and soon they were splashing their bare feet and giggling like schoolgirls. Longarm couldn't help wondering whether they were. He knew it was none of his infernal business. Running away from home was not a federal offense. So he tried not to ask questions—but in the end, of course, he did.

Their story was familiar. The two girls were cousins from a farming village farther east that sounded mighty stuffy, to hear them tell it. They'd managed to get mixed up in a scandal or two and the village elders had told them it was time they straightened their laces or carried on so awful somewhere else. So Flo and Becky had come west for adventure. That was what they called it: adventure.

Flo explained how they'd pooled their resources to buy the team and buckboard, then rode with it aboard a westbound freight to the boom town of Kanorado they'd heard so much about. There, she said, a mean old lawman had told them just to get out of town. He'd cussed them and said they weren't planning on holding amateur contests on the Ogallala Trail. Flo said she didn't know what he'd meant.

Longarm chuckled and said, "I figured Duke Watson was a man of the world. He may have cussed you, but he was giving you right fatherly advice, ladies. I don't give advice I ain't been asked for, but if you did ask me, I'd

30

suggest you stay away from Stateline, too."

He took out the modest wad of spoils he'd collected from the would-be toll takers and added, "Look, gals, there's enough here to get you both back home. If you tell Duke Watson I sent you, I'm sure he'll let you hang about Kanorado long enough to board a train to some neck of the woods less exciteful."

Flo reached for the money, grinning with delight. "Oh, goody, you can be our first customer! Which of us do you want to screw?" she asked.

Longarm blinked in dismay. "Hold on now, damn it. I'm trying to *reform* you gals, not buy your services. No offense, Miss Flo, but ain't you young gals a little young?"

Blonde Becky surely was. She was blushing furiously as her bolder companion said, "Pooh! How's a beginner to get experience if nobody will hire her without experience? We're both seventeen, and it's not like either of us is still a virgin, you know!"

Longarm smiled crookedly. "I wasn't trying to insult your skills, Miss Flo. But slap and tickle on the village green is one thing and servicing trail herders in a wide-open cow town is another matter entire. You kids are surely pretty enough and I reckon old enough, but, no offense, you don't look *tough* enough."

He saw that even Flo looked a little worried and Becky was already scared skinny, so he chose his words with deliberate brutality as he warned them, "A fancy gal in a trail-town cathouse don't get to pick and choose. She's expected to take 'em as they come, and some old boys come pretty rough after a week or more in the saddle. Half of 'em will be drunk and all of 'em will need a bath real bad. In the better houses they put a folded blanket across the foot of the bed so's the cow shit on their boots won't mess the sheets. The sheets get mussed like hell, anyways, after

31

six to sixty hard-up cowboys been on 'em and in the gal assigned to that particular crib. You ever take on that many men in one night, Miss Flo?"

Flo's expression was uncertain, but her voice was defiant as she replied, "Well, we did encourage our school team that time by offering to reward 'em with more than kisses if they beat Willow Bend. So it's not like we're afraid of a little fun." She giggled. "Becky was only game for five. She's always been shyer than me."

Becky covered her face with her hands and told Flo not to talk so dirty. Longarm found it sort of embarrassing, too, but now that he'd started their reformation he had to go on with it. So he laughed sort of nasty and said, "Shoot, the bitty schoolboys you took on wouldn't even make a real trail-town whore sweat. You gals ain't whores, you're just a mite warm-natured. You'd best go back East where men use soap and razors more. Look, I ain't saying you should behave yourselves *entire*. But I'd hate to see such delicate creatures roughed up by the sort of rascals patronizing trail-town business establishments."

Flo asked mockingly, "How would you see us doing anything? Are you a Peeping Tom?"

Longarm didn't answer. He'd done his duty, but some folk just wouldn't listen to advice, and this line of talk was giving him a hard-on. It must have been having a similar effect on the gals, because Becky, the shy-acting one, suddenly blurted, "I'll show you who don't know how to screw, you mean old thing!"

She must have meant it, for she proceeded to shuck her sky-blue dress with amazing speed and, as she did so, Longarm saw she'd been wearing nothing under it.

That wasn't all he saw. For such a skinny gal, dressed, the blonde had mighty big but firm-looking breasts. She lay back in the grass, closed her eyes, and spread her thighs.

32

"Well, you paid us, didn't you?" she asked.

Before Longarm could answer the brunette laughed wildly and said, "He's not man enough to take us both on!" But she must not have meant it, judging from the way she was shedding her own satin dress.

As Longarm watched, bemused, Flo stretched her own darker, plumper naked body on the grass beside Becky, keeping her eyes as well as her thighs open as she said mockingly, "You're the one who says it hurts to take on more than one at a time. So how about it, cowboy? Are you *scared?*"

Astounded would have been a better word to describe Longarm's feelings at the moment. But since his treacherous old organ grinder had already risen to the occasion, and he didn't want the sassy young things to call him a sissy, he tossed his cheroot in the creek, his hat in the grass, and said, "Powder River and let her buck!" as he proceeded to join them.

Since the blonde had started the challenge to his manhood, Longarm mounted her first, not wasting time on gentle foreplay, since she most needed a lesson in roughneck loving. She proceeded to screw him silly while the sassy brunette watched, commenting lewdly on their performance.

Longarm had noticed in the past that it was often the shy-acting ones who turned out to be the man-eaters. He wondered if the plump little brunette was as sassy with her well-padded rump as she was with her mouth. So when Becky moaned she was coming, Longarm pumped her over the edge politely, then rolled off and grabbed the brunette with no further ado.

As he flattened her back in the soft grass and wedged his hips between her softer thighs, Flo gasped, "Take it easy, damn it! I'm willing, but I bruise easy!" Then, as he entered her, or tried to, Flo's eyes widened in dismay.

"Jesus, Becky, you might have *warned* me!"

The blonde propped herself up on one elbow, still rubbing the pale thatch between her own thighs, as she said dreamily, "Isn't he hung swell? I don't remember anything that big as part of the home team, do you?"

Flo groaned. "No, thank God! That's deep enough, God damn it! I'm only a woman, not a cow!"

But Longarm figured she didn't really mean it when, once it was all the way in, Flo began to thrust with her broad hips and roll her head from side to side in the grass, moaning something about it hurting so good until she suddenly went crazy and came at the same time he did. Then he laughed and said, "Your turn again, Becky," and suited actions to his words by dismounting from the brunette and rolling over to board the blonde.

Becky protested, "Wait, I've already come!" as Longarm shoved her down and shoved it in her. He said, "That's all right. I have, too, but parties like this are sort of stimulating. I thought you gals wanted to be whores."

The blonde whimpered, "We do, but let a girl get her breath back, for God's sake!"

"Just pretend the herd's in town, little darling. I doubt like hell I can screw either one of you sixty times in a row, even if there was time. But you just had a good rest while I was servicing your business partner, so you ought to be able to satisfy one man between you."

She started to cry, calling him a brute. He knew he was being a brute and it was a lot of fun as well as needful. Having fired off his first round, Longarm found it easier to pace himself now. He was determined to save the real climax for the nicer one next door. He kissed her ear and tongued it to heat her more as he ran a hand down between them to play with her moist clit while he laid her.

As he'd hoped, it drove her wild. She gasped, "Stop that!

I'm already so excited I can't stand it and if you don't take your hand away, there, I'm going to...oh, I *am!*"

He laughed, rolled off and out of her, and told Flo it was her turn. But the brunette was crawling away on her hands and knees for her duds as she protested, "You didn't give us *that* much money, damn it!"

He crawled after her, caught her by the hips, and rose to his knees to thrust it in her dog style from behind, saying, "You're wrong, ma'am. How much did you gals figure you'd be paid a trick in Stateside? Cowhands only make thirty or forty a month, you know. So the usual rate's three ways for two dollars, or a quickie for six bits, and there must be more than twenty bucks in that roll you just got from me!"

Flo pressed her face to the grass and beat on the sod with her clenched fists, groaning, "You animal! This way's indecent in broad daylight with another gal watching!"

He kept humping her like a critter. "That's nothing to be shy about, honey, for I mean to screw her the same way, once I come in your sweet rump!"

Behind him, the blonde sat bolt upright in the grass and protested, "You'll do no such thing! Don't you have any *romance* in your soul, sir?"

He didn't answer. He was coming, and from the way Flo's back was arching to thrust her entry way higher, he knew she was, too, no matter how she cussed him and chewed grass.

Longarm cut Flo loose and made a grinning grab for Becky. The blonde leaped up and tried to get away, but he grabbed an ankle and spilled her to her hands and knees in the grass. As she tried to crawl away he grabbed her bonier hips and mounted her from the rear as well. He had a little trouble getting it in this time because of her fool gyrations, but his old organ grinder was smart as a cutting horse when it came to finding its way unguided. So when he felt the throbbing gates of paradise he just shoved his own hips forward, and damn, she felt tight, considering.

Becky sobbed, "Not in *there,* you dummy!" and he said, "Oops, sorry, " but added, you may as well get used to this way, now that I've arrived. I told you the good old boys would be expecting all three ways for two dollars, remember?"

She started bawling like a baby even though he was really treating her gentler than she figured to be treated in the near future if he couldn't mend her sassy manners. Flo jumped him from behind, rubbing her big naked knockers all over his sweaty back as she protested, "You son of a bitch! You're hurting her!"

Longarm said, "Don't be so impatient, Flo. You're next this way, and there's a third way we ain't even gotten around to yet."

Flo started crying too. He fired his last round in Becky and withdrew to roll into the creek and clean up as he cooled it off. He saw they were both grabbing their duds and asked, "What's wrong? I thought you gals was real pros. We still got plenty of time before we have to ride on to Stateline."

As he approached Flo, who was nearest, she covered her nudity with her gathered duds and said, "Don't you touch me! You're not a man, you're a freak of nature! Who ever heard of a man coming that many times in even *one* woman?"

Longarm pasted a puzzled smile across his suntanned face as he protested innocently, "Hell, we was just getting started. I couldn't have done more to you than even half a football team just now. We ain't been here long enough."

The once sassy Flo blushed beet red as she sobbed, "Damn it, we were only bragging on what the old biddies back home accused us of. We never really took on the whole

36

team—just the fullback and the boy who made the winning run."

Longarm said, "Well, I never! To think I believed you ladies when you told me you was on your way to Stateside to be fancy gals!"

Becky sobbed, "We've changed our minds. I'd rather wash dishes than get treated so mean!"

"I'm sorry," Flo said. "We're just not up to earning the whole twenty all at once. But can we keep some of it, at least?"

Longarm said they could keep it all, since it wasn't his in the first place. So the gals got dressed and the last he saw of them they were headed back to the railroad, not even waving back from their buckboard as they drove it north, sudden.

It made Longarm feel good all over as he got dressed to ride the other way. For it wasn't every day a man got the chance to lead an erring brother or sister back to the path of righteousness.

Chapter 4

There was no herd in town when Longarm finally drifted into Stateline late that night, so he almost missed the place in the dark. There wouldn't have been much to see there even by daylight. The town was little more than a wide spot in the Ogallala Trail. He followed the sounds of rinkytink piano until he saw the dim outline of a saloon door with one coal-oil lamp burning inside. He tethered his weary mount to the hitching rail out front and parted the batwing doors to see the place was empty, save for a barkeep reading a magazine behind the mahogany and a skinny old gent practicing at an upright piano near the back. The barkeep looked up and said, "We was about to close, friend, but I'll stake you to one drink if it's nothing fancy."

Longarm said he'd like a schooner of needled beer and some directions. "I'm in need of a telegraph station, a livery stable, and a hotel, in that order."

The barkeep filled his first order as he said, "Western Union's around the corner. Ain't no livery, but you can stable your horse in back if you're a guest of this here hotel, which you likely are, since it's the only one in town."

Longarm took the schooner in hand and washed down some trail dust. "That sounds fair," he said. "If this is the only bed and board in town, a gent called Tyrone Flynn must be staying here, right?"

The barkeep shrugged. "It depends on who's looking for him."

Longarm slid his open wallet across the bar, explaining that he was on Deputy Flynn's side, and the barkeep said, "Upstairs. Room 22. You want room 23, or are you unusually close friends with Flynn?"

Longarm laughed. "I'd best take the room next to his. His wife's jealous-natured. I got some luggage aboard my McClellan, but I'll pay up front if you like."

The barkeep said, "The room's a dollar a night, in advance. You can finish that schooner before you give me two bits for it."

Longarm didn't comment on the outrageous prices in Stateline. He'd known all along it was a trail town. He counted out the money on the bar and said he'd see about his mount and possibles after he wired home. The old gent at the piano turned to say, "I'd be proud to stable your horse and carry your things up to room 23, mister."

The barkeep said, "It's all right. I'll vouch for Windy. He plays lousy piano, but he don't steal."

Longarm nodded. So the old man followed him outside, where Longarm handed him a dime as well as the reins of his hired mount. Windy said, "Why, thank you, son. I'd have done it anyways, for another lawman."

"Oh? Are you the local law here, Windy?"

The old man sighed. "Nope. Not nowheres, nowadays. Used to ride for the Rangers, when the world was a mite younger and gayer."

He held up a hand in the dim light and added, "This is why. Comanche arrow did my hand in, years ago, down in the Staked Plains."

Longarm nodded soberly and said, "You still play a mighty fine piano, considering, pard."

Windy shrugged. "Man don't need no trigger finger or thumb, if he practices enough on the piano, I reckon. I'll let you in on a secret, in case you ever get your gun hand crippled. You just plays the chords with your left hand and hit the high notes one at a time with your middle finger, see?"

Longarm said he'd keep that in mind. So they parted friendly and, sure enough, there was a dimly lit Western Union office around the corner.

He went in and wired Billy Vail he'd made it this far, adding the brush with the saddle tramps and description of all but one. The gent he'd shot in the face could only be described overall, thanks to not having much of a face left.

As he handed his night letter form to the bored-looking clerk behind the counter, Longarm said casually, "I just rode down from Kanorado and I couldn't help but notice there were no telegraph poles keeping me company."

The clerk nodded. "That's 'cause there ain't no line north and south along this new trail. We just opened here, and such lines as we have run east and west to splice into the main network. Who did you want to wire in Kanorado? And, come to think of it, where the hell *is* Kanorado?"

Longarm laughed. "It ain't quite built yet. I was just sort of wondering how soon news could move north and south along the Ogallala Trail, is all."

The clerk looked wounded and protested, "Mister, we can send a message anywhere in these United States as has a telegraph office if we put our minds to it. Sometimes a message may have to go all the way to Denver or some other big town and back. But electric current zips along the wire so fast it hardly matters."

"I know how Morse code works. Used to send some, when I was scouting for the army. I doubt Kanorado has a Western Union office yet, though. Could you tell me how many other new trail towns might?"

The clerk shrugged and said, "Not right off. I'd have to wire the main office. I can if you want to pay for it."

Longarm said maybe another time and left to go back to his hotel. Windy had left for the evening and the barkeep, who doubled as room clerk, looked like he wanted to go to bed, too. He slid the key across the bar and said, "Your horse is bedded down with fodder and water. That'll be another six bits, by the way."

Longarm placed three quarters on the bar. The barkeep looked relieved. "I don't set the prices," he said. "I just work here. Your gear and saddle are up in your room. Will you be staying long?"

Longarm said, "Don't know. By the way, I'd feel better about my visit to your fair city if you didn't mention in the barbershop that I rode in with a badge."

The barkeep shrugged and said, "Ain't no barbershop yet. But you letting Windy see your badge was the next best thing to a barbershop."

"Oh? That why they call him Windy?"

"Yeah, he never shuts up. He was sober tonight, but you ought to hear old Windy when he's likkered and bragging on the Texas Rangers. He's full of shit, of course. More than one old lawman's caught Windy fibbing. He talks a convincing tale sometimes, but every once in a while a real lawman trips him up on the fine print. I reckon a gent like you could expose him as a blowhard fake in no time, right?"

Longarm said he didn't mean to try, since that would be disrespectful to his elders, as he picked up his key and went upstairs.

He saw a light under Deputy Flynn's door. He checked his own room out first, saw old Windy had piled his saddle and such on a corner chair near the big brass bedstead in the tiny room, and went back out in the hall to knock on Flynn's door.

He heard a muffled giggle, too high for a grown man like Tyrone Flynn to be making, and realized it might be a little late to come calling on a pard. He called out, "Never mind, Irish. It's me, Long, and we can talk about it in the morning."

He went back to his own room and shut the door. He was half undressed when he heard a knock. He pulled his pants back up, drew his .44 from the holster he'd hung over the bedpost, and went to open it.

Deputy Tyrone Flynn was shorter than Longarm but built strong as well as red-headed. Flynn had nothing on but a towel around his middle as he stepped inside, grinning sheepishly. He said, "Her name's Concepcion and she's a border Mex but mostly white. You want me to see if she has a friend, Longarm?"

Longarm said, "It seems you're all the friend she needs right now. How come you ain't carrying your sidearm, Irish?"

Flynn looked confused. "Hell, I knew who was in here, Longarm!" he protested.

The taller and wiser deputy said, "Meanwhile you've left your guns in the care of a lady of the evening, in a town where at least one deputy U. S. marshal has been gunned down by a person or persons unknown! God damn it, Irish, Pronto could have eaten you for breakfast, and his killer's still at large, and I find you traipsing around in the middle

42

of the night with no weapon but your randy pecker within reach!"

Flynn laughed boyishly and said, "All right, I'm dumb, and she don't really love me for my soul. Don't worry about old Concepcion. She just got here. It's my considered opinion that the rascal who killed Pronto Malone is long gone."

"You have any reason for such optimism, or did some little birdie tell you something you never saw fit to wire the office about?"

Flynn sat down on the edge of the bed, saying, "I wired Billy just this evening that the trail was colder than a well-digger's socks, Longarm. This town is deader than hell when no herd's passing through and you may have noticed, riding in, how few calves are bawling for their mamas tonight."

"Is it engraved in stone, somewhere, that townees never shoot up lawmen?"

Flynn shrugged his bare shoulders. "I've checked out all the locals. It didn't take much doing. The entire population wouldn't make a cavalry troop. Take away the women and obvious upright citizens and you're left with less'n a platoon of gents who even pack a gun. I took the liberty of wiring, discreet, about the few men in town who look mean enough to swat a fly. Come up empty-handed."

Longarm wasn't surprised. He said, "Damn it, Irish, we know old Pronto never would have let a *mean*-looking gent near him with that scattergun in broad daylight. So the killer has to be an *innocent*-looking cuss, and . . . Never mind. What's the story on brands you may have noticed when you wasn't riding Concepcion's range?"

Flynn chuckled and replied, "Don't knock her till you've tried her. Since I've been here, only two trail herds has passed through: Lazy M and Oxbow Slash. Both Texas outfits, known to be respectful of other folks' property. I

43

checked the brands by daylight, anyway. Nothing to report on either herd. They didn't even shoot up the town, passing through."

"Have you talked to any more witnesses to Pronto's killing?"

"Ain't been no more to talk to, Longarm. I've talked myself blue in the face to the half dozen who saw him going down under that cloud of shotgun smoke. Nobody got a decent look at the killer. I tell you, the son of a bitch is long gone, the trail's cold, and, what the hell, we was well rid of Pronto in any case."

Longarm raised an eyebrow. "Ain't Malone an Irish name?"

Flynn said, "There's Irish and then there's Irish. Pronto was a no-good disgrace to a royal race. We both know he would have been fired in a few days, anyway, had not he managed to get his fool self killed."

Longarm frowned and said, "*You* may know that, but *I* sure never. What makes you so sure the boss was out to fire Pronto?"

"Billy Vail wasn't out to fire him," Flynn said. "Billy was trying to save his ass by sending him out in the field until the heat died down. But it never. That she-male back in Denver got her gripe all the way to Washington and, well, you know Washington."

Longarm said, "I don't know what in thunder we're talking about here. Suppose you start at the beginning and use short words."

Flynn nodded and said, "The story is short and sweet enough. I guess you was out of town when it happened. Pronto was assigned to guard a she-male prisoner to federal court on a queer money charge. Her trial was postponed for later in the day. So Pronto took her to an empty office in the federal building and—well, you know how Pronto was, and they say she was pretty."

Longarm gasped. "Jesus! He couldn't have been dumb enough to compromise his badge with a woman prisoner! That's the first thing they teach us never to do!"

Flynn shrugged again. "He screwed her, anyways, atop an office desk. That's the one thing they agreed on. She claims he raped her. Pronto said it was a friendly invite. Billy Vail must have taken his word for it. He sent Pronto out on a field case, hoping it'd all blow over. It might have, had not he managed to get in all the newspapers bigger than life, as a dead man. They say the counterfeiting gal cut his picture out of the *Post* and sent it to her congressman. I'm surprised Billy Vail never told you any of that before he sent you here, Longarm."

Longarm said, "I should be. But Billy's covered for *me* in the past, so I understand his motives. The motive of the killer's still up for grabs. Counterfeiting can earn even a gal some serious time in the federal jug and, damn, why couldn't Billy Vail see that?"

Flynn chuckled. "He could. We talked about that angle back in Denver, discreet. The prisoner who accused him of mistreating her won't work. In the first place she was locked up tight in Denver the day Pronto got killed way over here. I suggested to Billy that the gal might have had a pal do it for her, but he said that made less sense for her to pull than just sticking to her story. The killing shut old Pronto up, so's he couldn't defend himself against her charge. But, on the other hand, it muddied the waters so much she's still in jail. By this time the Attorney General might have dropped the charges to whitewash the department. Now that Pronto's dead, it don't matter."

Longarm thought as he got out a couple of smokes,

handed one to Flynn, and struck a light, saying, "Yeah, the rape charge is literally a dead issue now. So there goes another likely suspect."

Flynn got back to his feet, thanking Longarm for the smoke as he added he had a border Mex spitfire smoldering some for him, too, next door.

Longarm did have a few more questions, but it felt silly talking to a man with a hard-on. He let Flynn go back to his Concepcion, locked his own door, and finished undressing to get in his own bed, alone. It didn't hurt as much as it might have, had he not taken the time to reform those wayward gals on the way down.

He was too tired to finish the cheroot he'd just started, too tired even to bother with the lamp. So he just snuffed out the smoke and rolled over on his face for some well-earned shuteye.

A lamp burning behind a window shade in an otherwise blacked-out trail town was a tactical error he'd regret before morning. But the Double Eight herd wasn't due in for a few more hours. So at least he'd get a *little* sleep.

Chapter 5

He was wrong.

A bullet crashing through a bedroom window at four in the morning was enough to wake anybody up, and Longarm was no exception. So he grabbed his .44 on the fly as he rolled out of bed and flattened on the floor as another round punched a second hole through the shade and sent more glass cascading to the floor. A voice from out in the dark yelled, "Rise and shine, you sleeping beauties! When the Double Eight is up, *everybody's* up!"

Longarm raised his left hand gingerly to trim the coal-oil lamp aboard the chest of drawers. A couple more guns went off outside, but no more lead came through his particular window, so he groped for his duds in the dark and commenced to dress below the level of his shot-up window.

He'd just finished when he heard Deputy Flynn pounding on the door. He rose and asked, "Is there a light on in the hall out there, Irish?"

Flynn said there wasn't, so Longarm opened the door to let him in. Flynn was little more than a blur in the darkness, so Longarm had to ask if he was dressed and where Concepcion was. Flynn said he had everything but his hat and boots on and that the Mex gal was under the bed. Then he asked Longarm why.

Longarm said, "Sounds like advance riders for the Double Eight. I was told they was headed north. They'll have their cows bedded on the grass to the south. Soon as it's light enough to tell a cow from a jackass, we'd best have a casual glance at their brands."

Flynn said, "Billy Vail don't have no Double Eight brand on his list of suspects, Longarm."

"That's all right, *I* do," Longarm said. "It occurred to me the minute I heard of cows branded with a Double Eight that it wouldn't take a genius to run a block-lettered 'U. S.' into two eights. You just heard what uncouth manners the outfit has."

Flynn whistled softly. "Hot damn! That stolen Injun herd *would* have been branded 'U. S.'! Let's go down and see what they has to say about bills of sale as well as manners!"

Longarm said, "Simmer down. No two lawmen born of mortal woman have any business confronting forty men or more in the dark, or even the light, if it can be avoided. Their ramrod is said to be a testy gunslick going by the name of Four Eyes. He wears specs. Ever heard of him?"

Flynn said, "No. He must not have been working on his rep long, for I'd surely recall mention of a gunfighter wearing specs. It don't sound natural."

Longarm moved toward the window as he snorted in disgust, "It don't sound natural for any man to desire a rep as a gunslick. But that's one of the things that makes this job so interesting."

He cautiously raised the shade. Nothing happened. He couldn't see much out there, either, but the light in the room improved some.

He said, "It's dawning, some, to the east. Does the hotel know about the gal in your room?"

"Sure. How did you think I found her? Why?"

"You'd best tell her to stay put for now, unless you'd like to share her with a mess of randy cowhands. We'll let that first bunch as rode in simmer down some. After sunrise, when the streets ain't so empty, we'll go down and join the festivities, casual-like."

"I follow your drift. I likes making love in the morning, anyway."

Flynn started to step outside. Then they both heard the sound of a piano starting up downstairs. Longarm said, "Damn! There go the best laid plans of mice and men! I got to shut that piano player up before he blabs about me to his new customers!"

Flynn said, "I'll back you," but Longarm said, "No, go lay Concepcion some more. Two strangers in a saloon cause twice the comment of one."

Knowing how the drovers downstairs would be dressed, Longarm left his frock coat and shoestring tie behind and headed for the stairwell in just his shirtsleeves and vest under his pancaked Stetson. He knew his hat gave him away as a Colorado rider and the exposed cross-draw gun rig wrapped around his hips might be considered a dare as well. But they'd hoorah him sure if he showed up dressed like a tinhorn or a preacher. Carrying a federal badge had been a mite more discreet before the reform administration in Washington had insisted on all federal employees dressing sissy.

He tried to saunter into the main room of the crowded saloon without drawing attention, but it didn't work. He could see at a glance that, save for the fancy gals who'd appeared by magic or women's intuition, every gent in the place was dressed cow and covered with trail dust. They could see at a glance that he didn't ride with them, but nobody said anything until Longarm edged over by the piano, where old Windy was tickling the ivories with more speed than skill. Longarm leaned over as if to request a tune. A ham-like paw grabbed him by the shoulder and spun him around as its owner growled, "Leave the professor alone, townee. *We'll* tell him what he's supposed to play, hear?"

Longarm smiled crookedly at the burly drover who'd laid hands on him and said softly, "Don't ever do that again, friend."

Another Texas accent in the crowd called out to one and all, "Hoo-haah, San Antone! Old Sandy's found him a *hee-ro!*" So, naturally, another hand laughed and shouted, "Hit him once for me, Sandy. I'm too busy with this gal in my lap!"

The one who'd started up with Longarm grinned at him and asked, "How do you want to play, pilgrim, fist city or for keeps?"

Longarm glanced down at the single-action Walker conversion Sandy packed and said, "I don't reckon we'd better play at all, Sandy. I'd be dumb to fistfight a gent with shoulders like yourn, and you don't look dumb enough to draw against a real gun with that antique on your hip. So why don't we just have a drink instead?"

"What's the matter, pilgrim, are you yellow?"

"Nope, just a grown man with a merciful heart. I can see my company ain't wanted here, so I'd best just leave this place to you and your pals, Sandy. It's been nice talking to you."

It didn't work. The loudmouth might have let him crawfish, since what he'd said about their sidearms was the simple truth and the bully didn't look like a suicidal maniac.

But as Longarm started backing for the stairwell to the strains of "Green Grow the Lilacs" a shorter, thinner gent wearing glasses and an S&W double-action in a low-slung buscadero rig nudged Sandy out of the way and said, smiling wolfishly at Longarm, "I'll handle this, Sandy. Go hold my place in the corner. It shouldn't take long."

Longarm sighed. "I sure wish someone would tell me what the hell the beef is, here. For I've been in Dodge of a Saturday night and nobody acted *this* surly."

Four Eyes purred, "What's happening here is anything we want to *say* is happening here, stranger. Didn't nobody never tell you the Double Eight drinks alone?"

"I got that message. I fail to see why I can't just leave peaceable. I've herded cows to market in my day, old son, so I know how wild and wooly a man can feel when he hits town after a mess of tedious days on the trail. But do we have to push this from hoorah to foolish?"

"You made a brag, mister," Four Eyes said. "You tried to back one of my boys down by intimating you could eat cucumbers and do wonders with that Colt you're wearing. Let's just say I'm a curious-natured cuss who'd like to give you a chance to show how good you are."

Longarm grimaced and said, "I can see what a chance you give a man, backed by a couple of dozen to witness for you if you win and avenge you sudden if you don't. I'm sorry, sonny, I'd like to help you build your rep, but I don't like to shoot men wearing glasses. So I'll be leaving now, and if you've got a lick of sense we'll be parting friendly."

He started backing further away, still smiling. Had Four Eyes let him, Four Eyes might have enjoyed a longer career as a budding bad man. But he said, "On the count of three!" and started counting. So Longarm drew when he got to two and Four Eyes died before he got to three.

Then all hell broke loose.

Longarm only put two rounds in Four Eyes, one over the heart and another for luck as he flew backwards into the crowd. Then Longarm shot out the two hanging lamps, plunging the saloon into dark chaos as he crawfished up the stairs, reloading.

On the second-story landing Deputy Flynn met him, gun in hand, to ask what the hell was up. Longarm said, "I'm heading up to the roof. You get that gal and your own ass somewhere else, sudden. They're only after *me* at the moment. Let's keep it that way. *Move,* Flynn, that's an order!"

He didn't wait to see if Flynn was obeying him or not. Boot heels were thudding on the stairs below and someone was shooting his gun off in the dark downstairs just for the hell of it.

Longarm went up to the third story. That was all there was. But a ladder at the end of the top hallway led to a trap door and when he shoved it open he found himself staring at a flat tarpaper roof behind the false front. He climbed out and shut the trap door. Then he cursed.

Save for the waist-high false front between him and the main drag, there was no other cover up here. The rooftops on either side were too far away to jump across to. He was trapped. The sky to the east was pearling pink. He didn't even have his Winchester and damned near every rider for the Double Eight figured to have a long-range saddle gun at his disposal.

He whirled and raised the .44 in his big right fist as the trap door popped open. Flynn called out, "Don't shoot. I brung our Winchesters."

Longarm said, "Bless you, my child. Where's the girl?"

"Slid her down the back wall on knotted sheets. What's the story up here, Longarm?"

Longarm helped him out of the trap door as he growled, "See for yourself. You should have lit out when you had the chance. We're in one hell of a pickle up here, old son."

Flynn looked around, shrugged, and said, "Well, there's no cover for anyone on them other rooftops and nobody can shoot us from the street or prairie, out back."

"They won't have to," Longarm said. "This is a frame building and at least one of them pissed-off Texicans has to have a match!"

Flynn said, "Oh," and hunkered down with his back to the false front, both Winchesters across his knees.

"Give me my saddle gun," Longarm said. "I suppose asking about the local law would be a dumb question?"

Flynn handed him his Winchester. "They have a copper-badge town marshal, here. He homesteads about six miles out of town. They say when the herds is in town he has some gardening to do. The townees don't figure to help us, Longarm."

"I said it was a dumb question. Next roof is about twenty feet off with a three-story drop between. Reckon you could make a running jump that far?"

"Hell, no. What about you, Longarm?"

"I doubt it. But who knows how far a man can leap with his ass on fire? Wish this roof was wide enough for a good long run at her."

Flynn cocked his head and observed, "It sure is *quiet*, this morning."

Longarm listened. "Yeah. Nobody run all the way up after us after all. The survivors likely run back to the main outfit to get help. Damned if I can see why. They must be sissies."

Flynn asked if he knew how many gents they might be talking about. Longarm took out a couple of cheroots, handed one down to Flynn, and said, "Can't say for sure. Most big market herds are drove by forty to sixty riders. A dozen or more either way won't cut much ice when they hit us. You do have a full magazine in that Winchester of yourn, don't you?"

"Sure. It was peaceable as hell around here until *you* showed up!" He suddenly squinted and added, "Damn! The sun-ball just showed up, too!"

Longarm didn't bother turning to look. He could see it was daybreak as he peered over the top of the false front at the dusty, deserted street out front. He took a drag on his smoke and observed, laconically, "They're taking their own sweet time, considering how simple any plan they can come up with has to be."

Flynn took a deep drag, let half of it out so his voice wouldn't crack, and asked quietly, "You reckon we're done for, Longarm?"

Longarm shrugged and said, "Everybody's done for, sooner or later, if he lives to be a hundred."

"Yeah, I'd planned on dying sooner or later, but this is sure sooner than I'd have chosen, had it been up to me," said Flynn.

Longarm didn't answer. There was nothing to say.

They smoked in silence for a time. Then Flynn suggested, "If they all rode back to their camp, what's stopping us from just opening that fool trap and sort of sneaking down and out?"

Longarm said, "If they're that dumb, we got nothing to worry about."

"Oh, right, a couple of gents forted up on a stairwell would be in a nice position to pepper one's ass on a ladder. But it's sort of getting on my nerves, just setting here."

"You go on down if you've a mind to, Irish. If you don't

get shot in the ass I'll join you, hear?"

"I wish I felt so jolly this morning, you big grinning bastard."

Longarm shrugged and said, "I wouldn't exactly say I felt jolly. But grown men ain't allowed to cry, so what the hell. Heads up, I hear someone riding in from the south!"

Flynn rose and they both braced their Winchesters over the top of the false front to stare thoughtfully down at the three riders coming down the center of the dusty street. The older-looking one in the middle rode a big black stud and carried a big white flag of sheeting. Longarm let them ride within carbine range, but when they got within tolerable pistol range he shouted, "Hold her right there, gents!"

The mounted trio reined in. The man on the black stud called out, "Don't shoot. I'm Silas Webber, owner of the Double Eight, and I come to jaw with a gent calt Longarm about the killing of my ramrod, Four Eyes Bronson."

Longarm called back, "You found him, Webber. Who's been taking my name in vain?"

"The old piano player mentioned you in passing as he bolted out the door. How come you never told my boys who you *was*, God damn it? They never would have started up with a gunslick with *your* rep!"

"I had all that figured out already, Webber. What happens next?"

The cattle baron handed his flagstaff to a sidekick. "I've been studying on that," he said. "I'll lay all my cards face up for you, Longarm. I'm peeved as hell at you for gunning my ramrod. On the other hand, I got a big herd to drive a long ways and I suspicion I'd play hell making her all the way to Nebraska after gunning a federal deputy. So I'm leaving your heated discussion with old Four Eyes up to his kin back home, if it's all the same to you."

Longarm nodded and said, "That sounds fair. I got lots of kinfolk mad at me already, so one or two more won't matter. I told your fool ramrod before I shot him that I wasn't looking for a war."

Webber replied, "So be it, then. Permission to bury our dead?"

"Permission denied. He'll keep down there in the cool saloon until at least noon. You were planning to ride on before then, weren't you?"

"My herds been watered and rested and the boys say they never seen such an unfriendly trail town, so, yeah, there's nothing keeping us here now. Come on down and we'll drink on her."

"Not hardly. We'll just stay up here while you move on through. Make it soon, for I get moody as hell on a hot day with no shade and it's fixing to be a scorcher."

"Oh, hell, Longarm, I just told you the war's over, didn't I?"

"You did, and I'm too polite to call a man a liar unless I'm sure of his intentions. But we'll still stay put until you and yourn ride on, if it's all the same to you. Don't worry about bodies we can bury just as well, unless you aim to leave some *more,* hereabouts."

Webber cursed under his breath and wheeled his mount around to ride back to camp. Longarm had been right about it figuring to be a hot day. The sun was higher and the tarpaper roof was baking him and Flynn by the time they saw a mess of cows moving past town to their east under a billowing cloud of dust. Longarm lit another cheroot and said, "Looks like the grass over yonder's about grazed off at the roots. It sure ain't clear, from here, how many brands might or might not have been run in recent memory."

Flynn shrugged. "Old Webber seems sort of sensible," he said.

Longarm said, "I noticed. No sensible gent would want a brush with the law if he was herding stolen cows, and if Four Eyes wasn't a hired gun he was just plain loco. As soon as it's safe to go down to the telegraph office we'd best wire the office. Billy Vail can likely put someone closer to them brands between here and Nebraska, now that we've learned the rascals some manners."

They waited almost another hour. Finally Longarm said, "Well, if they left anyone behind to settle scores, we ain't about to meet him up on this fool roof. I'll go down first, You cover me."

Nothing happened as he dropped to the hallway below. Flynn followed as Longarm covered the stairwell. They played leapfrog down to the main saloon without incident.

Once there, they found the barkeep, old Windy, and a gent in a black suit drinking at the bar as they regarded the corpse on the floor near the piano with distaste. The barkeep said, "This here's the coroner or dentist, depending, Longarm. We was waiting for your permit to drag this son of a bitch out of here so's I can open for business again."

Longarm stepped over to stare morosely down at Four Eyes. Flynn did, too, and said, "Jesus, you sure messed this one up, Longarm! What in thunder did you put through his fool head, a sledgehammer?"

"He was wearing glasses. Soft-nosed .44 slug hitting a pair of specs at the bridge, and dragging 'em on through, do make a mess, don't it?" Longarm said ruefully.

"That's for damned sure. I was figuring to check him out on the recent wanted flyers. But we'll have to take his word for who he was, now."

Longarm said, "He ain't been posted for anything serious. I'd have remembered the glasses. He was just a fool who read too many Wild West magazines and didn't get the joke." He turned to the coroner. "Uncle Sam will pay for planting him, if you don't bill him for silver handles and such. You got any papers for me to sign?"

The dentist said he hadn't had them typed up yet. Longarm nodded and said, "I've time to send me some wires, then. You know where to find me when you're ready for my John Hancock."

He went outside. Flynn didn't surprise him by following, but old Windy did. Longarm asked why he was tagging along and the piano player said, "Thought you could use some help. I used to be a Ranger, you know."

Longarm didn't comment on that. He'd already told Webber he hated to call a man a liar unless he had to. As they headed for the Western Union office the old man babbled away about all the cases he'd solved in his day. Nobody paid much attention until he got to, "I offered to help that other deputy. The one as got kilt. But he just laughed at me, sort of mean. I reckon he was sorry I wasn't backing him the day he met that jasper with the twelve-gauge. I knows everyone in these parts. So I might have been able to warn him, see?"

Flynn muttered impatiently, "Windy here says he saw the killing." He didn't sound like he believed it, but Longarm had learned how often wisdom sprang from the lips of babes and boobs. "Is that right, Windy? Did you witness the killing?" he asked.

Windy said, "Well, sure, I tolt everyone I did, didn't I? It was right back yonder in front of the saloon. I was inside, fixing to start playing for the evening crowd, when, wham, bang, two mighty shotgun blasts rung out!"

Flynn snorted. "See what I mean?"

Longarm asked, "How could you see a killing in the street if you was in the saloon, Windy?"

"Easy," Windy said. "I wasn't setting at my piano. I was having me a drink at the bar, near the door. I couldn't see out entire, of course. Them batwings was in my way. But when I heard the shots I naturally turnt, and saw the *legs* of both of 'em. Then Deputy Malone's whole body flopped down into my line of vision. So I knowed I'd heard something serious. The killer run north, cutting around the corner of the building, like them others all said."

The two deputies exchanged glances. Flynn nodded. "It works. The other witnesses were on the far side of the gunsmoke. So they only spied a hazy figure through the considerable cloud."

Longarm asked Windy, "Are you sure the killer was a man, Windy?"

The old man blinked in surprise. "Thunderation, what *else* could it have been? I ain't blind. I can tell a he from a she in broad daylight!"

"Yeah, but you only saw the killer's legs and feet."

"I did indeed, and that's how I know he was a man. I've heard of she-males wearing pants agin the laws of nature, but she-male feet don't come that big. The gent as shot that other deputy wore raggedy jeans and low-heeled boots. Army black, they was, and big enough to steam up the Mississippi. No gal has feet that big, even in low heels."

Longarm filed the clue away, if it was a clue and not just an old windbag trying to sound important. The late Four Eyes had been wearing high-heeled Texas boots and spurs. He had an alibi for Pronto's killing in any case, since he hadn't reached town yet at the time.

They went into the telegraph office and Longarm let Windy bend Flynn's ear for a spell as he jawed with the clerk behind the counter. This one was friendlier than the night man and was able to tell him that, yes, a telegram could be sent from here to the new trail town of Kanorado to the north, going the long way around. He had a wire for Longarm from the home office, too. Longarm opened it, saw Billy Vail was just fussing at him for gunning those saddle tramps, and put it away. Then he sent Vail a longer one, bringing him up to date, suggesting someone take a closer look at the Double Eight herd between here and Nebraska, and then, trying to keep it polite enough to send over a public wire, chided his boss seriously for not filling him in on the trouble Pronto had had back in Denver and requesting more information on possible enemies of the dead lawman. He added that he couldn't seem to find anyone in this neck of the woods who'd fit, even with Flynn's help. He hesitated, then passed on what Windy had said about the killer being a big-footed gent in jeans and low-heeled army boots, adding that it was an unconfirmed rumor, so far. Then he told the home office to wire their answers back to him care of Western Union at Kanorado and told the clerk to send it collect, day rates. It was Billy's own fault for holding out on him about Pronto being in trouble before he ever got to the Ogallala Trail, bless his devious hide.

The three of them left the telegraph office and had breakfast at a beanery down the main drag. Windy hadn't been invited and Longarm figured he'd have to pay for the old man's chili and beans, but when they finished the old man paid his own tab. Maybe he was just lonesome after all. Longarm was too polite to ask how much they paid him for playing piano with eight fingers.

Back at the saloon, the body had been carried out and the barkeep had sprinkled fresh sawdust where he'd oozed into the floor a while. The dentist—coroner was still there, still drinking, but he had a statement for Longarm to sign, typed up. Longarm read it. It didn't have any very important facts wrong, so he signed it and bought the coroner a drink when he agreed that was all he needed.

He couldn't buy Windy a drink because the barkeep cursed the old man and told him to get cracking at the piano.

So Windy was playing "Up in a Balloon" too hard to listen in as Flynn said, "I'll keep an eye peeled for a big-footed gent in low-heeled boots, just in case. But I still think he's full of it. He says he used to be a lawman, too, but I caught him on not knowing the difference between a sheriff and a marshal."

Longarm shrugged. "Well, Ned Buntline's Buffalo Bill books ain't too clear about the distinction, neither. You gotta admit he surely lost his trigger finger and thumb to something wild out West."

The coroner drinking at his other side told Longarm, "That's easy. Everyone in town know how he lost them fingers. He told us, just before he decided he'd been a Texas Ranger fighting Comanches. He used to work in a lumber mill. Figure it out from there."

Flynn grimaced. "Like I said, just an old windbag. What's our next move, Longarm?"

Longarm said, "I'm riding on up the trail, unless you gents can show me someone here in town dressed in ragged jeans and big low-heeled boots."

They both looked blank. He nodded. "That's what I thought you'd say. If Windy really saw anything, it ain't here now. But I ain't had a look at many boots in Kanorado yet."

Flynn asked when they were leaving and Longarm said, "You ain't. Billy Vail put you here to check brands and there'll be more herds coming up the trail. Be careful when the Rocking X comes through. The Richardson brothers are high on Vail's suspicion list and I'll be switched if I can see what's keeping them this long. I'll keep in touch with you as well as the home office by wire. You see any brands as could have been run from a 'U. S.' to anything at all, get word to me no matter how fresh the brands look, hear?"

"I will, and Concepcion thanks you. But I can't see how

you'd run a blocked 'U. S.' to a Rocking X, mean as the Richardson boys are said to be."

Longarm put down his empty schooner and said, "That should make it easier for you, then. Wake me up around noon, will you?"

"Wake you up? Ain't you already up, Longarm?"

"Not really. And the Double Eight just left. I can travel faster on foot than a herd of cows on their way to market and I don't want to catch up with that outfit on the lone prairie. So I may as well get me some beauty sleep."

Chapter 6

Longarm managed to go upstairs and get back in bed without cutting his feet on the glass all over the floor, but it seemed to him he'd just dozed off when he awoke again to see a pretty Mexican gal staring down at him. She was seated on the bed, on the politer side of the sheet he'd hauled up over his naked hide. She even had some clothes on, sort of, if a low-cut peasant dress and skirts up around her knees qualified as proper attire. Longarm scowled up at her and said, "If your name's Concepcion, old Irish is a pal of mine and, no matter who you are, how did you get through that locked door without waking me up?"

She said, "I work here, so I have a key to all the rooms, *señor*. I am not that *puta*, Concepcion. I am called Estralita. I do not give myself to men for money."

He propped himself up on one elbow, admiring the view over the top of her low-cut blouse more from this angle. "Well, now that you're in here and we've established you

63

ain't no fancy gal, what *do* you want from me, Miss Estralita?" he asked.

"It is said you are riding up to Kanorado, *es verdad?*"

"I might be, later. Is there something you want me to deliver for you in Kanorado, ma'am?"

"*Si, señor*. Me. I have to go north to Kanorado, *muy pronto*, but there is no stage line and I am afraid for to ride alone on your big empty prairie."

"That's the first sensible thing you've said. But I dunno, Miss Estralita, I ain't in the travel business and, to tell you the truth, you might be safer alone than anywheres near me. Someone on the Ogallala Trail's picked up a bad habit of gunning federal deputies, of which I'm one. Can't you get anyone else to carry you north?"

She swallowed a brave little sob. "No. That is why you must take me with you. I have to get there soon, for to do something most important. There is money in it for you, if that is what you want."

He wondered how the employees of this ramshackle saloon hotel managed to get so rich on what the place could be paying, but it was none of his business. So he smiled and said, "I don't charge nobody but the Justice Department for my services, Miss Estralita. But before you clouds up and rains all over me, suppose you tell me what's so important to you about this trip north."

"I can't. It is a secret. But I will do anything, *anything*, to get to Kanorado!"

She must have meant it, for a big old tear ran down her velvety brown cheek as she leaned closer, letting him see more of her chest as she gave him a free sample of her musky perfume. She smelled like sweaty jasmine mixed with she-male. He tried to ignore the effect it was having on his glands as he asked her gently, "Are you in some kind of trouble here in Stateline? You can tell me. I'm about the biggest gent in town right now."

She shook her head, spraying his bare shoulder with teardrops as she replied, "No, I have done nothing wrong here, I swear. The owners know I have to leave. They have paid me. They will not be angry at you for taking me with you. But you *must* take me with you to Kanorado!"

He shook his head. "I'd like to. I can't. I'm on a case for the Justice Department and, to tell the truth, one old deputy I used to know just got his fool self in trouble messing with a she-male while he was supposed to be working for Uncle Sam."

"Por favor!" she pleaded, moving even closer. "Is there any law against a *caballero* escorting a *mujer* safely through Indian country?"

"Not exactly, and it ain't exactly Indian country, lately. But, all right, I'll spell it out for you, Miss Estralita. It sounds to me as if you're up to something."

"I have done nothing wrong! I swear this on my mother's grave!"

"Yeah, and naturally you'd be honor bound to tell a known lawman the truth if you had. Let's see, now. You can't be ducking the border patrol, this far north. I'd remember if a pretty little Mex gal had held up a bank or a train, recent. What are you carrying on you, stolen goods?"

Her brown face paled as much as it could manage and she made the sign of the cross as she protested, "Oh, what are you accusing me of, *señor?* I have no stolen goods in my possession! You can search me if you like!"

He chuckled. "That surely sounds like fun, Miss Estralita, but simmer down. Us federal agents don't mess with hotel silver and such in any case. I'd have heard if anything serious enough for Uncle Sam to worry about had been stolen hereabouts. So you just get up to Kanorado as best you can and we'll say no more about it. Lock the door with your pass key on the way out, will you?"

She did no such thing. Bawling like a baby, she proceeded to tear her clothes off as she called him a brute for suspecting her of criminal tendencies. As he got a good look at what she'd had concealed in her clothes all this time, which was only her brown curvaceous hide, he said soberly, "You sure must want to go to Kanorado, Miss Estralita."

Before he could stop her she slid under the thin sheet with him and gasped, "Oh, I do! I do!" as she pressed her warm flesh to his, including the part that was making a liar of him as he protested, "Now hold on, Miss Estralita!"

She must have taken his English literally, for she grabbed his erection and held on tight as hell, pleading, "Please do not refuse me, *Señor* Longarm!"

He rolled his eyes heavenward and muttered, "Well, I tried, Lord, but a man has *feelings*, you know!"

It felt nice as hell when he rolled Estralita under him, shoved a pillow under her brown rump, and she locked her soft brown legs around his waist and sighed, "Oh, *que grande y que bonito!* I am coming with you to Kanorado, *si?*"

"Well, I know *I'm* coming, soon as hell, if you keep wriggling like that, *querida.*"

"*Si*, me, too, it has been so long since I have been with any man at all and...*ay, caramba*, I really *am!*"

That made two of them, unless she was faking, of course. But if she was, she faked such a fine orgasm with her internal muscles that he was willing to forgive her. Whether he wanted to take her with him on the trail was another matter entire. But meanwhile, since he didn't go anywhere *else* for a spell, he decided to come in *her* some more.

But they'd barely gotten good at it before Flynn pounded

on the door to tell Longarm it was high noon.

Longarm announced that he was wide awake, which was the simple truth, and when Flynn clomped off he asked Estralita if she had her own pony. She said she did, so he told her to slip out the back way discreetly and meet him on the prairie north of town in about an hour. As soon as she'd left he got dressed, picked up his saddle and possibles, and went downstairs looking innocent to ask what he owed for the keep of his mount out back. The barkeep said he could settle up with the colored kid who tended the stable.

Longarm found the young boy sleeping in the haypile and would have left him to his sweet dreams had not he noted his hired gelding had been curry combed as well as fed and watered handsome. He saddled the critter, then he woke the boy up and handed him a quarter. The kid looked sleepy and astounded, in that order. He thanked Longarm profusely and added that not many gents staying at the saloon hotel tipped him at all.

Longarm asked him why, in that case, he took such good care of the horses. The boy smiled shyly and said he liked horses and that had he not been birthed with such a dark complexion, he'd have liked to be a cowboy.

Longarm smiled down at him and said, "You've got some growing to do, pard, but once you fill out some, I foresee a future for you in the cattle industry. Try landing a job as a wrangler first. Most sensible outfits are color blind if a man can cook or take care of their ponies good. After they get used to you, practice in front of the ramrod with your throw rope and wait till he invites you to a roundup. I've met more'n one colored top hand in my travels."

The boy grinned and said, "I reckon you rode for the North in the War, right, suh?"

Longarm shrugged. "I disremember which side. The War was a long time ago. I've met lots of Indian cowboys, too,

67

and our racial discussion with *them* was even more *recent*.
Don't talk like that when and if you apply for a job chasing
cows. Most folks don't think too much about what a man
might or might not be unless he beats 'em over the head
with it."

The stable boy looked abashed. "That's what my mama
told me, suh. I'm sorry. I wasn't thinking. You see, a gent
who stayed here a few days back calt me a Big N, and I'm
still a mite pissed."

Longarm said, "Some men are like that. I wouldn't call
'em *gents*." Then he frowned and asked, "Few days ago,
you say? Was this mean-mouthed man in town when that
deputy from Denver got gunned out front?"

The stable boy thought and said, "As a matter of fact,
he left that very evening, suh. Calt me a useless nigger son
of a bitch 'cause I hadn't saddled and harnessed his bay
mare. How was I to know ahead of time he wanted his old
mare? Nobody told me."

"He do sound impatient, don't he? Tell me something,
pard. Was this gent wearing ragged-ass jeans and low-heeled
boots?"

"No, sir, he was dressed in a suit, like you, only fancier.
He looked like a tinhorn gambler. Only they say he didn't
deal cards in the saloon while he was here, just checked in
for a day or so and rid on."

Longarm thanked the boy for the information, led his
gelding outside, and mounted up to meet Estralita, still
pondering the stable boy's tale of a mean-mouthed, fancy-
dressed drifter with no visible means of support.

The Mexican gal was waiting for him north of town
aboard a painted pony, riding bareback with nothing but a
carpetbag across her lap in the way of luggage. As they
rode on together he asked Estralita if she knew about the
fancy-dressed stranger who'd been staying at the hotel in

Stateside the day Pronto Malone was murdered. She looked down and said she remembered the gent and that he'd stayed in room 27. She said she didn't recall his name.

Longarm asked her why she was blushing so and Estralita allowed the dude had acted mighty foreward with her, adding something about a wrestling match across a bed before she could get loose and leave him to make his own damned bed. Then she changed the subject. Longarm made a mental note that whatever reason she had for leaving town in such a hurry had to have come up since then, unless the fancy-dressed dude was downright hideous.

Longarm had no false modesty about his own looks. It would have been impolite to question the word of all the ladies who'd admired him in the past. But common sense told him that a gal who'd leapt into bed with him willingly, might well have given in to a more persistent cuss, if she'd wanted to go north so bad the day of the killing.

Estralita kept urging him to hurry, but he told her he wanted to reach Kanorado well after midnight, since the Double Eight would likely be there. She gave up arguing about it after a while, and when they came to the cottonwood draw he'd rested in with Flo and Becky, she was a good sport about shading from the hot afternoon sun.

The green grass he and those sassy gals had crushed was standing tall again but the creek was running drier now. It would likely dry up entirely between now and the next rainy spell. Prairie creeks were like that. Meanwhile, there was still green grass and water, so he turned their mounts loose to graze under the trees and suggested Estralita might like to cool off in the shallow water.

She was a good sport about that, too. She stripped herself bare and proceeded to wallow in the sandy creek like a contented brown pig, albeit built a lot nicer. It inspired Longarm to shuck his own duds and join her. The water being far too shallow for swimming, they wound up engaged in other water sports. She damned near drowned him when she got on top, but it sure was fun.

They finished sensibly in the sweet green grass, and Estralita answered another shocking suggestion with a gentle snore. Longarm was still wide awake. He let her sleep and took the opportunity to search her carpetbag.

He didn't find anything incriminating. He lit a smoke and reclined contented beside her, pleased to see he wasn't as big a fool as the late Deputy Malone, after all.

He was still glad Flynn hadn't seen him ride out of Stateline with a possible suspect. *He* knew the difference between compromising his badge and innocent fun, but the distinction wasn't always so clear-cut. He blew a thoughtful smoke ring as he wondered some more how Pronto Malone could have let himself get into such a silly mess. Pronto had been a cheating husband and a man who carried skirt chasing past all common sense. But he'd still been an experienced lawman, damn it. With a sheepish grin, Longarm could recall chasing more than one skirt past common sense, himself. But he'd never in a hundred years have messed with a woman prisoner.

Yet Pronto's defense to her charge of rape had been an admission he'd laid her willing, right in the infernal federal building. Longarm shook his head and muttered half aloud, "That counterfeiting gal must be some looker. For Pronto was in a position where he should have said no thanks to Madame Sarah in the bare-ass flesh!"

He tried to think of a gal handsome enough to tempt *him* into such a foolish move. But no such woman existed, even in the *Police Gazette*. Pronto couldn't have been likkered up. The dead deputy had had a lot of vices to answer for, but he hadn't had a drinking problem. As a matter of fact, looking back on the few times they'd worked together, old

Pronto had been as reliable as most, on the *job*. And even if one allowed he'd lost his head with the counterfeiting gal in Denver, he'd been gunned in Stateline by someone else entire.

Longarm saw he was thinking in circles and dropped it for now. He finished his smoke and would have taken a nap in the grass beside his pretty traveling companion had not Estralita suddenly awakened and, seeing him flat on his naked back with his eyes closed, proceeded to wake him up, she thought, with a French lesson. He rose to the occasion and returned the favor for her as she giggled and said his moustache tickled. They took another bath together after, and after he'd made her come in the creek she even let him sleep for a few hours. But after sundown Estralita woke him up again, less polite, and insisted she had to get to Kanorado.

He bought some more time by breaking out some cold grub he'd picked up in Stateline. Then they screwed some more, had another bath, and bade *adios* to the hidden prairie Eden.

Chapter 7

The full moon was getting high when Longarm and Estralita came to where he'd had it out with the self-appointed toll collectors. He didn't see any bodies. Someone had tidied up after him. But the fence they'd strung was still there, flattened in the grass. Obviously the Double Eight had passed this way some time before.

They rode on, Estralita complaining about getting to Kanorado so late. He tried to cheer her by pointing out that if they didn't have a hotel built there yet it was a fine dry night and he had a sleeping bag in his saddle roll. She hesitated and replied, "I cannot stay with you in Kanorado, *querido*. The people I am meeting there would not understand. I shall never forget you, but you know how my people are."

He nodded soberly, too polite to say he knew only too well how some old Spanish-speaking boys felt about his kind messing with their she-male kin. He'd been wondering how he was going to get rid of her, in any case.

A spell later he heard a distant high male voice, singing sad and lonesome about not wanting to get buried on the lone prairie. He told Estralita, "We'd best swing wide and follow the railroad tracks in from the west. Unless that's a sleep-walking lunatic up ahead, it's a cowhand picketing a herd bedded down for the night. Damn, I was hoping the Double Eight had finished their beer and moved on by now."

He led Estralita west by moonlight until they were well inside the state of Colorado. Then he took a bearing on the North Star and they rode on until they hit the tracks and the telegraph line. He led her over the tracks and then they followed them at a walk until they saw the lights of Kanorado ahead. He said, "Yep, they're making a night of it in town, sure enough. We'd best bed down out here on the prairie, honey. Riding into a wide-open trail town with a pretty gal ain't sensible even when you haven't just shot the ramrod of the outfit making all the noise."

But when he reined in, Estralita said she had to meet her friends sooner than that. So he considered the odds, shrugged, and said, "Well, if you got backing and a place to stay, it's likely safe enough. Make sure you keep to the darker lit streets and enter by the back door."

She rode closer to kiss him *adios*. He let her, then, as an afterthought, asked, "By the way, how do you know so much about Kanorado? When I passed through just a short spell back, they'd barely started building the place."

Estralita said her friends in Kanorado had wired her they had a place for her to stay now. "They said the city is already two blocks long," she added.

"I noticed they was hammering pretty good. If we meets in town, *mañana,* which seems mighty likely in such close quarters, I ain't to act as if I know you, right?"

She sighed and said, "*Si,* alas. That is the way of my people."

So they kissed again and parted friendly. He waited until she'd vanished in the moonlight before he rode north another mile to lay his roll on the dry grass. Trains going by any closer could disturb a man's sleep some.

He watered his gelding and hobbled it to graze and went to bed on the ground with his Winchester. It wasn't built as nice as Estralita, but it was comforting to have in his arms just the same. He took off his hat and boots, balled his gun rig and frock coat for a pillow, but left his other duds on for the same reasons. Then he went to sleep.

He was awakened at dawn by the sun in his eyes and a horny toad licking ants off his ear. So he sat up, scaring the ants and horny toad even more than they'd scared him.

His mount hadn't run off in the night and the can of tomatoes he opened cleaned the sleep gum from his mouth good enough. As he sat cross legged on his bedroll, eating tin-flavored tomatoes, he heard cows bawling in the distance. When he gazed to the east a cloud of dust was blotting out a lot of the otherwise clear prairie sky. He nodded, crushed the can and buried it under some sod scalped free with a boot heel, and put his gear back together to ride on in.

As he got to Kanorado, he saw Estralita's pals had wired her wrong. The mushrooming town was now even bigger. He heard hammering in the distance that explained why.

But though the business district had grown some since his last visit, the closest thing to a livery in Kanorado was a corral next to the railroad depot. The depot itself hadn't been there last time he'd looked. So he put his gelding in the corral with the others, telling it to just sit tight and there'd likely be a roof over it by the time he got back.

He packed his saddle and possibles over to the main street, looking for some place already built to leave them. He met Duke Watson first. The town law now wore a frock

74

coat newer than Longarm's and sported a mail-order copper star on his lapel. Longarm said, "Howdy, Duke. You boys sure work fast. I'm looking for a hotel or at least a bar to hide this gear behind."

Watson fell in beside him. "I'll be only too proud to show you to the best whorehouse in Kanorado, since I happens to own stock in it," he said. "Ain't sure the fancy gals is ready to serve *other* services just yet, though. We just had a herd in town and the ladies need some beauty sleep."

Longarm chuckled. "Yeah, I noticed the Double Eight was as wild an outfit as you warned me."

Duke said, "Don't be so modest. We heard about you and Four Eyes down Stateside way. Remind me never to lock horns with you, Longarm. I'm paid to be tough, too, but gunning a ramrod in front of his crew is tough to the point of lunacy! How in thunder did you come out of that alive, pard?"

Longarm shrugged and said, "Always shoot out the lights, after. I see you has more hair on your chest then the town law in Stateside, so I got a question to ask you. Did you get a good look at any Double Eight brands by the dawn's early light? I've a good reason for asking."

Watson nodded. "I know. I got the all-points your office sent out yesterday. I can't say I examined every cow, but I looked more'n one over as they moved out at dawn and if old Webber's run any U. S. brands recent, they surely heal fast on the trail."

He led Longarm across the road to a mustang-colored frame house with lace curtains in its windows. A hardcased-looking gent at the door said he'd be proud to take care of Longarm's gear and suggested he come back later in the day when the ladies were more rested.

Longarm owed the town law for the favor. He asked

where the nearest drinking establishment was. Duke pointed with his chin at a pair of swinging doors across the street and said, "That's the only saloon in town as is open yet. Tell 'em I sent you and they won't water your drinks so much. I can't take you up on your kind offer just yet. It ain't seemly for the town law to be seen drinking on duty in a place he owns a half interest in."

Longarm laughed and said he'd buy him one later, when he got off duty. Then he asked, "Which way is your Mexican quarter, Duke? I got reasons for avoiding that part of town just now."

Watson frowned and said, "We ain't got no Mexican quarter here in Kanorado. Hell, there's barely enough room for *white* folks here!"

Longarm frowned, then shrugged and muttered, "Well, I reckon a lady's entitled to her secrets. If we ain't drinking, could you point me at your Western Union?"

Watson told him it was down at the far end of the short main street. They parted friendly and Longarm went to see if the home office had anything to say to him. On the way he passed a gunsmith's shop and that reminded him he could use a box of .44-40. But it could wait till after Western Union.

The clerk inside had two wires for him. One long wire from Billy Vail had been sent as a night letter. The other, shorter message had just come in a few minutes before, day rates, so Longarm opened it first.

DEPUTY FLYNN SHOT IN BACK THIS MORN-
ING BUT STAY WHERE YOU ARE STOP FLYNN
UNCONSCIOUS BUT EXPECTED TO LIVE AND
ON WAY BACK TO DENVER STOP WITNESSES
SAY FLYNN SHOT BY RIDER FOR ROCKING X
IN STATELINE AND HERD IS HEADED YOUR

WAY STOP DO NOT TRY ANY ARRESTS ON
YOUR OWN STOP POSSE ON WAY TO KANOR-
ADO AND SHOULD BEAT ROCKING X STOP
VAIL US MARSHAL DENVER DISTRICT
COURT.

The long formal signature meant Billy Vail was serious
as well as mighty pissed. Longarm was pissed, too. He
picked up a pencil stub and wired back:

I OWE IRISH STOP WITH OR WITHOUT BACK-
ING ROCKING X AINT GETTING PAST ME
STOP CUSTIS LONG DEPUTY US MARSHAL
DENVER DISTRICT COURT AND I MEAN IT.

He handed the message to the clerk and asked what time
the next train from Denver was due. The clerk said, "It
ain't. Hadn't you heard? There was a train wreck last night
near Limon Junction. Highball freight ploughed into a string
of cattle cars some idjet switched wrong. Tracks are blocked
with a quarter mile or more of wreckage."

Longarm muttered, "Shit." The clerk, who'd taken down
the message from Vail, scanned Longarm's message to Vail
and asked, "Do you still want to send this, Deputy Long?"

Longarm nodded grimly. "Go ahead. I hardly ever wire
lies to my boss."

The clerk observed that he was either brave as hell or
stupid and moved to put it on the wire as Longarm tore
open the night letter, saw it was only a rehash of the trouble
Pronto Malone had gotten into in Denver, and put it in his
coat pocket to read later. It was starting to look like he
might need *two* boxes of extra ammunition, now.

In the brand new gunsmith's shop he found a tall brown-
headed gal behind the counter. She was waiting on a cus-

tomer ahead of him. Longarm stood politely gazing down at the shooting irons in her glass case as he waited his turn.

The gent was wearing a black frock coat and a pearl-gray Stetson that looked like it had never been stomped on yet. He was standing in fancy, spurred high-heeled boots. So Longarm dismissed him, or would have, had not the stranger's voice been so annoying and know-it-all. As Longarm listened, the other customer told the gunsmithing gal, "Money is no object, miss. I'll tell you what. I'll raise my offer to a thousand dollars cash on the barrel head!"

A thousand dollars on or off a barrel head was a serious amount of money. Longarm perked up his ears as the gal gasped and said, "But, sir, this model revolver's not worth anything *like* a thousand dollars, even *new*, and, as I told you, Colt Arms has discontinued the line. I'd be only too happy to sell you a matching gun for much less. But I just don't have any way to *obtain* one for you."

Longarm moved casually closer to get a look at what they were talking about. He saw the gent's gun on the counter between them. It was a long-barreled silver-mounted Navy Colt .36 conversion with carved ivory grips. It was pretty as hell, but not the sidearm of a serious fighting man. The man who wanted another one said, "All right, you have me in your power, ma'am. I'll raise my offer to fifteen hundred dollars. But, I'm sorry, that's as high as I can go!"

The girl looked astounded. "I assure you I'm not holding out on you, sir. I told you before, the gun you want a mate to is a presentation model, made in limited numbers while Mr. Colt was still alive. They just haven't made any guns like that since Seventy-four at the latest. I can sell you a nice presentation Peacemaker with ivory grips, if you like."

"Don't be silly, my good woman. I'd look ridiculous wearing a Navy conversion on one side and a Peacemaker on the other."

Longarm couldn't resist saying, "When you're right you're right, mister. But the lady's right about that model, too. I've never seen a handsomer shooting iron than that'n. But wouldn't it make more sense to just wear two fancy *new* guns? No offense, but that presentation piece is left over from the War."

The stranger smiled thinly and said, "I know. I carried it through the War for the Army of Virginia, sir. The companion to it was stolen from me recently and I mean to replace it. You might say I'm attached to this model for sentimental reasons. You're both right about it being a presentation piece. The late Sam Colt presented it to my late father before the War. So money is no object—within reason, of course."

He turned back to the gal and asked, "What does your catalogue say a gun like this is worth?"

She said, "I told you before, sir, it's not listed in Colt's recent catalogues. Without the silver mounting and ivory grips, I could probably get a Navy .36 like that for you for less than twenty dollars." She brightened and added, "Oh, that's an idea. What if I ordered a regular model from a used gun shop I know of further east and had it custom trimmed and gripped for you? I could swing the whole deal for no more than two hundred dollars."

The man shook his head. "I've seen the sort of custom work they do these days. Look at the patina on that carved ivory. That's inlaid sterling silver, too. The coin silver they use these days would never match, even if the engraving was as fine. But surely this can't be the only such gun Sam Colt ever made."

She shrugged and said, "I doubt they made more than five hundred of that particular presentation at the most. This is a cow town, sir. The men I usually do business with buy and sell more functional arms as a rule."

"But you do buy guns as well as sell them?"

"Of course. I often take a damaged gun in trade to fix and, well, sometimes a boy finds out by the time he's ridden this far north that he doesn't really need two guns as much as he needs drinking money. But, heavens, you could hardly expect a cowhand to bring in a fancy gun like *that* one!"

The stranger picked up his treasure and holstered it in one of the two holsters he wore under his frock coat. "I'll be leaving town when they get that train wreck cleared away," he said. "But I'll drop by again just before I leave. Remember, though, no more than fifteen hundred dollars!"

He grumped out on his high heels, silver spurs ringing. The gunsmith gal turned to Longarm with a weary smile. "I hope you don't want a matching set of gold-inlaid Murdoch dueling pistols, sir."

Longarm chuckled. "Nope. Just a couple of boxes of .44-40, ma'am. I hardly ever duel with Scotchmen."

She raised an eyebrow and said, "You do know something about guns, don't you?"

"Long, Custis Long, ma'am. I rides for Uncle Sam, and he hardly ever lets me fight duels with flintlock Murdochs. But I read some, so I know how the upper crust used to live."

She said her name was Fanny MacLogan and came around the end of the counter to get at the ammunition on a high shelf across the shop. There was a stepladder handy, but she just reached up natural for what he wanted. He figured she had to be almost six feet tall, but as she stretched in her summer print dress he could see she was built winsome enough for such a big gal. He glanced down at her feet. They were bigger than most gals' feet, but she wore high-heeled high-buttons of light tan kid. So there went a notion that had sounded sort of dumb in the first place.

She moved back around the counter to make change as

he paid her for the ammo and pocketed it. He waited until his lawful business there had been completed, then he said, "This likely ain't my business, ma'am, since selling gold bricks ain't a federal offense. But I'd better warn you, anyways. That rascal with the tale of riding for Virginia in the War is out to skin you."

She looked worried and puzzled at the same time as she asked him, "How? He wasn't trying to sell me a gold brick or anything else. He was trying to *buy* a gun I just don't have, for an astounding price!"

"I was astounded, too, ma'am, until I remembered how it worked. They usually pull it in jewelry stores. But there ain't no jewelry store in town and I can see it working just as well with a gunsmith."

"Mr. Long, I wish you'd get to the point."

"Call me Deputy Long, if Custis sticks in your throat, Miss Fanny. The con is usually pulled with matching jewels, for higher stakes. But he looked sort of tinhorn to me, so mayhaps his needs are more modest. Do you agree it's just silly to pay fifteen hundred dollars for an old shooting iron, pretty or not?"

"Of course. But *I'm* not supposed to pay that price. *He* is!"

"So he just said. Meanwhile, you're primed to make more in one sale than you'd likely make in weeks, if only you could get your hands on a silver-mounted Navy Colt with ivory grips."

"Of course. But I don't know where in the world I could get my hands on such a rare revolver, Custis."

Longarm chuckled and said, "Just sit tight and one ought to be walking in any minute, ma'am. He said he was leaving town soon, as I recall."

She looked at him as if she thought he'd been out in the hot sun too long. He added quickly, "His confederate should be coming by in a while. Said confederate will be an innocent, dumb-looking cuss down on his luck with a gun he wants to sell for quick cash. Said gun will naturally be a silver-mounted Navy conversion with ivory grips."

She frowned and asked, "Why would he want his friend to sell me such a gun if he's looking for such a gun, Custis?"

"It'll be the same gun, of course. You're supposed to notice what a swell match it is and swindle the poor, broke confederate shameless. How much would you be likely to offer for a gun you think you can sell right off for fifteen hundred dollars, Miss Fanny?"

She said, "Oh, I guess a fifty percent markup would be fair. . . ." Then she caught on and gasped. "Oh, what a mean trick!"

He nodded. "I know of one jeweler, back East, who laid out ten thousand for a matching earring he aimed to sell for twenty. It was worth about four thousand, tops. Naturally the customer willing to buy it for his upset wife who'd lost it at the opera wasn't really a guest at the fancy hotel address he gave. So the con artists made a clear profit of six thousand for a few minutes' work. Ain't folks greedy?"

She sighed and said, "Clever, too. That gun was really valuable, albeit hardly worth more than a few hundred dollars. What are we to do now, Custis?"

"Nothing," he said. "Con men hardly ever hurt folks. So when the confederate comes in with the same infernal gun, you can just say you ain't interested, and they'll go somewheres else to try it on another."

"I'm frightened!" she said. "I've been held up in the past and even though I have a loaded revolver under the counter, I've never had the nerve to use it. Won't you stay until the other one comes, please?"

He started to say he didn't have time. But how fast could anyone drive a herd of cows up here from Stateline? He likely had at least a day to wait for the Rocking X and, what the hell, she was prettier than any schooner of needled beer. So he said, "I can stick around, some. Might be a good notion if I went out the front and come in the back, in case they're watching."

She was learning fast. She moved to unlock the rear entrance as Longarm stode out the front, waving back at nobody at all, and moved down a few buildings before he stepped into a slit between them to take a leak, a shortcut, or something.

Fanny let him in from the alley side. He saw he was in her quarters as well as her shop, now. The whole place wasn't big enough to swing a cat in, so he had to walk around her four-poster as she led him toward the front. He stopped just inside the curtains closing her quarters off from her sales room and said, "I'll sit here, on this bentwood chair, and catch up on my reading. I can hear good through drapes."

She nodded but asked, "What's our plan when and if?"

"We play her by ear," he said. "If he leaves quiet when you tell him you don't know where in thunder you'd sell such a gun or, better yet, offer him less than it's really worth, we'll just say no more about it. If he acts mean, I'll just step out and act meaner. I doubt I'll have to. Like I said, they're con artists, not stickup artists."

"Aren't you going to arrest the confederate, Custis?"

"No, ma'am. I ain't got jurisdiction on such petty matters. Once we know who they both are, I'll mention their manners to old Duke Watson and he can run 'em out of town, or whatever."

The bell over the front door rang outside, so Fanny had to go out. Longarm sat down. It was a townee in need of new hard rubber grips after using his shooting iron as a hammer. As Fanny fixed the fool's mistreated gun Longarm took out Billy Vail's night letter to read.

It was long, but not too interesting. After chiding Longarm for chiding him, and reminding Longarm of the time *he'd* been sent out of town after punching a Colorado state senator, good reasons or not, Vail allowed he'd hoped the heat about Pronto would die down as he inspected brands on the Ogallala Trail, but that it hadn't worked out well at all. The counterfeiting gal had been set free by the Attorney General for lack of evidence. That was what they called it when they had dirty linen to wash: lack of evidence. Said counterfeiting gal had naturally been shadowed with considerable interest after leaving the federal lockup, but had not been dumb enough to contact anyone and had last been seen boarding the stage for Golden, over by Lookout Mountain, northwest of Denver. The law in Golden said she'd reformed, at least as a queer passer, and was currently working in a house of ill repute as an honest whore. The bank in Golden was keeping an eye on its cash flow just the same and would wire Denver the moment any queer ten-dollar silver certificates turned up.

Longarm put the night letter away. It seemed safe to scratch the reformed counterfeiting gal as a suspect, since there was no way in hell she could have gunned Pronto or anyone else since she'd been arrested.

The bell outside tinkled again and Longarm nearly wet his pants when he heard a familiar voice saying, *"Por favor, señora, do you buy used pistolas?"*

He got up to peep through the curtains. It was Estralita and she had a silver-mounted Navy Colt conversion in her hot little hands. He muttered, "Perfidity, thy name is she-male!" as the two gals outside went through their song and dance. Estralita seemed sort of upset when Fanny offered her twenty dollars cash for the old gun. It was more than Longarm would have. Estralita said she had to think it over and lit out like a scalded cat, still in possession of her boy-friend's bait.

As soon as she'd left, Fanny parted the curtains with a laugh, almost bumping noses with Longarm. She didn't move back as she said, "You'll never believe it. It was a shy-looking little Mexican girl."

Longarm said he'd noticed. Then, since standing so close breathing in each other's faces seemed sort of awkward, he figured he had to either step back or kiss her. So he kissed her.

Fanny kissed back in a way that told him why she hadn't made the first backward move. But as they came up for air, she gasped and said, "Oh, dear, how did *that* happen?"

"Ain't sure. Let's try it again."

Fanny stiffened. "The front door's not locked, you silly!"

Since they were hidden from the front door by the drapes and it hardly took any time at all to stop just kissing, he wondered exactly what she had in mind. But he just asked, "Do you want me to come back later, after you close?"

She blushed and said, "You're awfully fresh. I should be mad, I suppose. But it's not every day a man saves a poor widow woman from being swindled."

He'd already known he'd saved her from being swindled, so he knew she was anxious to explain her status as a gal with no gent likely to walk in. But he could see she was delicate-natured despite her size, so he said, "If I ain't been shot by sundown I'll just drop by and see if you're receiving company this evening."

She blanched and asked, "Good heavens, who's liable to shoot you before sundown? You just told me those con artists were harmless."

"They are, even if the Mex gal tells fibs she ought to be ashamed of. I'd best level with you, Miss Fanny. A fellow deputy was gunned this morning in Stateside and I've reason to hope the gent as done it is headed this way, with a mess of backing. It might not be a good idea for us to get too close, now that I study on it."

So she kissed him again, hard, and told him she'd be expecting him for supper and that she closed around sundown.

He was starting to want her for supper, too, now that they'd rubbed against one another some. But he shook his head wistfully and insisted, "You putting a time and place in an uncertain future proves my sorry point, Fanny. You're inviting a tumbleweed to be in a certain place at a certain time. I just can't say where I'll be at sundown tonight. I've an appointment with someone uglier who ain't told me when he might or might not show up. Aside from which, win or lose, you got to stay here in Kanorado, after. Some of your more regular customers might not cotton to you being all that close with the law, see?"

She didn't take her arms off his shoulders and he noticed her long legs allowed her to rub against him sort of shocking, where it mattered to both of them, as she said, "You know the way to my rear entrance, Custis. I'll leave a light in my window for you and if you show up too late for supper . . . we'll think of something to do."

A bell rang, and it wasn't the one over her shop door. He'd already let one insistent gal make a fool of him on the Ogallala Trail. Little Estralita had suckered him with sweet talk after getting that wire from the cuss she'd said she hated so much, telling her to join him here in Kanorado on sinister business. He couldn't help wondering what sinister business this taller, prettier gal had in mind. What she was rubbing against him so insistent was too good to be true.

He said he'd try to make it back in time for supper or whatever, and they kissed again before parting friendly as hell.

Chapter 8

Longarm went first to visit his horse at the town corral. Sure enough, the hostler there told him a prissy-dressed dude and a Mex gal on a painted pony had recently eloped to the north. This didn't surprise Longarm much. He considered going after them, for more than one notion fit Estralita and her other lover boy. The con man had been in Stateline when Pronto bought the farm. Pronto had been a skirt sniffer who might have been lulled into a trap by a sassy hotel maid. But after that it sort of fell apart. Despite his brag about riding for Virginia, the con man hadn't struck Longarm as a killer, and why would Pronto have gone to meet a hotel maid in the street out front, instead of up in his infernal room?

Longarm considered wiring all points about their ingenious scheme. But the Justice Department didn't pay him to mess with petty crooks. So he chalked Estralita up to experience and went into the depot to ask how the railroad was coming with their wreck up the line.

The stationmaster said they were working on it and that the tracks would be clear by sundown. Longarm thanked him, even though sundown was shaving it mighty close. He was a day's ride north of Stateline. Cows moved slower. The backup Billy Vail was sending him would move faster by rail, but they had a lot farther to travel and at best couldn't get here any earlier than eight or nine that evening, even if the stationmaster was right about the new timetable. There was nothing he could do about it, so he went to have breakfast.

He was eating steak and spuds in the beanery when the town law, Duke Watson, caught up with him. Duke said it was all right to drink beer in a beanery, so Longarm bought him one and asked if they had a jailhouse built in Kanorado yet.

Duke said he had a patent cell as would hold three or four in the back of his office down the street. Then he naturally asked Longarm who he wanted held and for how long and how come.

When Longarm told him about the shooting of Flynn and the pending arrival of the Rocking X, Duke blanched and said, "Sorry. I feels for you but I just can't reach you, Longarm. We just built this town to *service* the trail herds, not to *arrest* 'em! Aside from it being bad for business, it would be suicide as well to go agin the Richardson brothers!"

Longarm washed some steak down with his own beer and said, "Hell, they ain't *both* headed this way. Only Reb Richardson, the elder and more sensible brother."

"You know what you are, Longarm? *Loco en la cabeza,* that's what you are! There's no such thing as a sensible Richardson brother. They just consider old Reb a mite calmer 'cause he talks meaner and don't kill folk as often. But he's kilt enough, and I don't mean to be no part of his score!

You can't stand up to him alone, Longarm. For he won't *be* alone!"

Longarm shrugged and said, "I heard words to the same effect about Four Eyes Bronson, as I recalls."

Duke snorted. "Beginner's luck. Four Eyes was ramrodding for a sensible boss. Reb Richardson *is* the boss of the Rocking X, and he picks his hands for gun as well as roping skills. You can go and get your fool self kilt, if you've a mind to, but leave me and mine out of it, hear? I'd run you ought of town to keep the peace, if I had the authority over your badge. But since I don't, I reckon I'll just go jackrabbit hunting till you leaves town. *Adios,* you idjet!"

When Longarm was alone with his breakfast again he finished it. Then he looked at his pocket watch. It wasn't even noon yet and if this was to be his last infernal day on this earth, how was he to kill it in such tedious surroundings?

The whorehouse would be open for business by now, but he'd never been able to make that mental adjustment, being sort of romantic-natured.

He considered going back to the gunsmith shop to see if old Fanny felt like closing earlier than usual. But that would be unfair to the big gal in more ways than one. So he went to the saloon instead.

He didn't want to drink too much. He found a poker game going in the back room and after he'd watched a while a tapped-out nester gave Longarm his seat at the table.

The game was penny ante and sort of tedious besides, with nobody trying to cheat. Longarm never cheated at cards against innocent stockmen and nesters. So he just sat there winning a few and losing a few for a couple of hours. Then a gent dressed cow but wearing an oily smile and a big, flashy finger ring came into the back room to stand about, looking innocent, until a cowhand who'd been losing said he had to get back to his chores at the spread and gave the stranger his seat, bless them both. For, as soon as the stranger had the deal, Longarm saw the game was about to get more interesting.

The new dealer dealt himself losing hands at first, of course, as he marked the cards with the mechanic's ring he sported. A nester who should have known better than to play cards with such an open face was naturally dealt a flush and happily raked in the modest pot. The game got tedious some more as Longarm got the deal, noted the markings, and just dealt straight for now. When it was the mechanic's deal again Longarm was not too surprised to find he had a full house. He acted dumb and raised the modest ante, expecting to be beaten by the not-so-mysterious stranger. But he won the pot instead. So he knew what had to be coming next. The card shark smiled friendly as a polecat in a henhouse and said, "I reckon this just ain't my day, gents. But, to make it interesting, what say we raise the ante to...oh...a dollar?"

Two townees dropped out of the game on the spot, but Longarm said, "Suits me. But hold the thought. I got to take me a leak before we settle down to serious card playing."

He went outside, stepped over to the bar for another schooner, and asked the barkeep quiet if they carried Flora Dora decks. The barkeep said they carried all brands of decks and sold Longarm the same Flora Doras as they were dealing in the back room at the moment. Longarm left his schooner on the bar and went back to the gents' room. He took a leak, since he was there, but then he got to work on the new cards, marking them with the same scratches, but not the same way. Then he went back in to rejoin the game. It was fixing to be an interesting afternoon, after all.

The card shark was too slick to try to wipe everyone out right away. As Longarm expected, the rascal kept everyone winning and losing modestly as the pot got bigger. By now word had gotten about and some more serious card players drifted in to watch the fun or join the game. Longarm was braced for some heated words when one of the earlier players won a fair amount and announced he was quitting while he was ahead. But the card shark just dismissed him with a friendly but contemptuous little smile and, sure enough, another sucker dropped right into the empty chair while it was still warm.

The card shark dealt Longarm another winning hand. He was already ahead of the game. So he knew the slicker had noted his string tie and had him down as the richest gent at the table. He wasn't too surprised when the rascal passed the deal to the newcomer and waited till the farmer was dealing clumsily before he smiled at Longarm and said, "You must be lousy with women, for you're lucky as hell at cards, friend."

Longarm shrugged modestly as he picked up his awful hand and said, "Not this deal, I ain't. I'm out."

The card shark said, "I'm not, and I raise." So, naturally, he lost, but took it like a good sport and suggested, "What say we make this game really interesting, boys? I have to meet a lady later, and as you see I'm way the hell behind. Only way I can see to break even in the time left would be...oh, let's say five dollars ante?"

He lost a couple of customers sudden, but Longarm said it was jake with him. So the card shark said, *"Bueno.* It's your deal. Be gentle with me, will you, pard? The lady I mentioned has expensive tastes."

Longarm said, "Wait a second. Got to check the time. I got to meet someone, too."

Naturally everyone there kept a sharp eye on his right hand as he fumbled the watch out of his vest. So naturally nobody was looking too close at his left hand as he switched the marked decks. He put his watch away and said, "Damn, it's later than I figured, gents. So I'll say up front that, win or lose, this is the last play for me and mine."

Then he dealt the slicker a straight flush and gave himself what would have been four of a kind, had the original markings been there for the cuss across the table to read.

The slicker never batted an eye as he looked at his cards. "I'll stay with these and raise," he said.

So Longarm raised too, as a greenhorn with a good but not as good as possible hand was supposed to.

The card slick raised again and added, "Are you really leaving us after this play, pard?"

Longarm looked at his cards, as if tempted to ride his luck some more, as he replied. "Don't want to. *Have* to. I raise."

Everyone else at the table but Longarm and the pro dropped out. So it was one on one when the man who thought they were playing with his own marked deck said, "I'll tell you true, these cards ain't so bad, and I'm still way behind. If you're fixing to leave with all them winnings, how's about being a good sport and making the ante twenty?"

Longarm hesitated, or seemed to, as he studied his own cards. Then he said, "Well, just this one time, so's you won't call me a sissy. I'll raise you twenty and, hell, let's go for broke. I'll raise you a hundred even."

Everyone in the back room whistled. The card shark tried not to look like he was coming in his pants as he raised again. Then Longarm called.

The card shark spread his straight flush on the table, saying, "Sorry about that, but I said the lady has expensive tastes."

But before he could rake in the considerable pot, Longarm said, "Hold it. Don't a royal flush beat a straight?"

The card shark stared across the table at Longarm's cards as if he expected them to buzz a tail and strike. He gasped.

92

"How in hell did you do that! You had four of a kind, damn your eyes!"

He realized his mistake at once and tried to cover by adding lamely, "I mean it stands to reason you had less'n a straight. A royal comes once in a blue moon, and..."

"I follows your drift," Longarm said, adding with a thin smile, "If you mean to accuse me of something, mister, just do so and cut the shilly-shally. Like I said, I can't stay here much longer."

He could see the stranger was considering hard. But the stranger could read death in another man's eyes as good as he read marked cards. So he shrugged and said, "There's always another day, if only a man can manage to live long enough. You win, friend. How come you're so lucky?"

Longarm raked in his winnings. "The angels watch over the pure and innocent, I reckon," he replied. Then he pocketed the considerable amount and stood up, adding he was springing for drinks all around. So they all went out to the bar to let him do so.

Longarm was consulting his watch again when the card shark sidled up to him at the bar and muttered, "Pretty slick. I admire your disguise and, now that it's over, would you mind telling me how you did it without a mechanic's ring?"

Longarm smiled. "Trade secret. I didn't catch your name, pard."

"I'm Doc Perkins. I thought I knew all the boys in the business."

"I ain't in the business. But a carnival gal I shacked up with one time taught me a few things. My handle is Custis Long and I ride for the law when I ain't indulging in minor vices."

Perkins gasped. "Jesus Christ! I took on *Longarm* and I'm still *alive?* I reckon my luck was with me today, after all!" He hesitated and added, "We're straight with one another, ain't we, Longarm? I mean, I never commented public on the way you switched decks on me in there."

Longarm chuckled and said, "We're straight, Doc. What you may have heard about me and that gambling man in Denver was more personal. He wasn't just a card shark, he was a wanted murderer. I know you ain't, for I've a good memory for yellow sheets. Your record says you was let off on grounds of self-defense that time in Waco. Is that why you're working so far north now?"

"Yeah, the rascal had kin who tended to disagree with the coroner's jury," Perkins said. "I figured it was better for all concerned if I left Texas."

He sipped at the beer Longarm had bought him, then lowered his voice even lower to say, shamefaced, "If we ain't to be enemies, I surely have a favor to ask of a *friend*, Longarm."

"We ain't enemies, Doc. What's your pleasure?"

"Uh, you tapped me out. I mean, all the way. I was sure, back there, I had you, so..."

Longarm nodded and asked, "How much do you need to get to the next town up the trail and get in a luckier game, Doc?"

"Could you spare me fifty?"

"Not hardly. But if you can't build twenty back up in no time you ain't a real gambling man."

Longarm reached in his coat pocket, found a twenty-dollar gold piece by touch, and handed it to his victim discreetly, adding, "I'd leave as soon as I finished that beer if I was you, Doc."

"Are you running me out of town, Longarm?"

"Nope. It ain't my town. But the boys will be expecting someone to buy the next round of drinks, and it ain't going to be *me*, this time."

Perkins looked relieved. "You're a decent cuss, for a

94

lawman, Longarm. I'll take your well-meant advice about this saloon. But I really do have a lady waiting for me at the boarding house and we can't leave town until the rails are fixed."

"Oh? Ain't you riding the Ogallala Trail north, Doc?"

"Not hardly. We've been working west, towards Denver. Why?"

"Just wondering. If you've come west out of Kansas, you couldn't have been in Stateline a few days ago." He reached in his coat again and brought out a fistful of money, saying, "Here, take this and git, Doc."

"I thought you said you couldn't stake me much, Longarm."

"I thought you was traveling alone. A woman stuck with a gambling man needs this money more than I do. When you two get to Denver, don't try dealing in the Black Cat or the Silver Dollar. Some of the regulars are meaner than me about mechanics' rings."

Doc Perkins said he'd remember that and they shook and parted peaceable if not friends. Longarm waited until he was gone before he went in the gents' room again and discreetly counted his winnings. He was still a couple of hundred dollars richer than he'd started out with. He made a neater roll of the bills, put the coinage in his pants, and went back out to see what else he could find to occupy some time.

He found a skinny little cuss with a copper star pinned on instead. Duke Watson must have described Longarm to his deputy, for the skinny cuss came right up to him and murmured, "Reb Richardson just rid into town. Duke thought you'd like to know."

Longarm looked at the wall clock over the bar with a frown and said, "That's sure quick marching for a herd of beef."

The town deputy said, "The herd ain't here yet. Richardson rid in ahead with two of his hands. They're over at the corral, admiring hell out of your horse, Longarm."

Longarm nodded and said, "That's the trouble with Western Union. They lets anybody wire anybody. I thank you kindly for your words of cheer and I'd best see what they have in mind. I don't reckon you'd admire keeping me company as I stroll down to the corral, eh?"

"Not hardly, Longarm. Duke said to tell you you're on your own."

Longarm said that sounded fair, said *adios* to his new pals in the saloon, and went out the back way, just in case. But as he approached the town corral a few minutes later he saw three gents dressed Texas leaning casually against the rails, staring his way thoughtfully.

Longarm walked over to them, stopped at conversational range, and said, "Afternoon, Reb," to the bigger, meaner-looking one in the middle.

Opinion was considerably divided on which of the Richardson brothers was the meanest. Some said Tex, the one who wasn't present, was less given to blowing off steam than old Reb, here. Longarm knew Reb better. They'd locked horns in the past. But since they were both still alive, he had some hopes of avoiding a real showdown if only he could keep the conversation civilized.

He couldn't. The big Texan said, "The one on my left is Spike and the one on my right is Noodles. They only rode in with me to keep me company, Longarm. This beef is betwixt you and me, private."

It wouldn't have been polite or diplomatic to call Reb a liar in front of his friends and backing, so Longarm smiled and asked, "What beef might that be, Reb?"

"Don't mince words with me, Longarm. You know one of my boys gunned that nosy deputy, Flynn."

"I did hear words to that effect, Reb. Is the man who gunned old Irish present, here?"

"Hell, no, I sent him home to Texas, after. He was just a kid. He wouldn't have stood a chance agin you."

"Is that why he shot Irish in the back, Reb?"

"It never happened that way, damn it. We had our herd grazing well out of town. Flynn rode out, early in the morning, looking for God knows what. He was pussyfooting about our cows when one of my riders mistook him for a cow thief and shot him fair and square."

"In the back," said Longarm, adding, "That's not a question. It's a plain fact."

Reb shrugged. "Now where in the U. S. Constitution do it say a cow thief is entitled to a fair fight? *I'd* have called the son of a bitch, had I been the one as seen him fooling with my beef so sneaky. But I wasn't. And my hand was following standing orders. So what's it gonna be, Longarm?"

Longarm said, "I'm still studying on it, Reb. What do you reckon Flynn was looking for when he trifled with your cows so foolish?"

"How the hell should I know? If you're talking about that government beef missing from the Osage Strip, it's a lie. I got me a bill of sale for ever' damn cow in my herd. You want to see 'em?"

"I hardly ever read fiction as a pastime, Reb. Mayhaps we'd best just wait until your cows get here and I'll just look their brands over myself."

Reb looked shifty. "They ain't coming this far north. We decided to sell 'em off in Texas after all."

"Do tell? How come you started 'em for Nebraska, then? Trying to run the fat off 'em for the cheaper southern market, Reb?"

"Don't play mealy-mouthed kid games with me, Longarm. You got some accusings to make, I'd like to hear you make 'em here and now, hear?"

Longarm nodded. "I'll tell you true, Reb. We did get a tip some Indian beef might have gotten mixed in with yourn by accident or something. Flynn was looking for run U. S. brands when your hand gunned him. Since he's in no condition to talk, and your herd's headed back to Texas, what we has here is a sort of moot question."

"Are we square, then?"

"Ain't sure. Maybe I'd best read your bills of sale after all."

Reb hauled a sheaf of greasy flimsies from a hip pocket and handed them over, saying, "Read 'em and weep. I was half tempted to tell you to fish or cut bait, but I'm a sensible, civilized cuss at heart."

As Longarm started leafing over the carbon copies of the bills of sale Reb added softly, "I still think I could take you."

Longarm ignored the brag as he read on until it got interesting. Then he handed the papers back. "I see you bought some beef off the Double Eight, Reb. I'd heard you and the Double Eight didn't get along too good."

Reb shrugged again. "Oh, I had a run-in with their ramrod, Four Eyes Bronson, but we kissed and made up. You can ask him. The Double Eight's headed north this season, too, I hear."

Longarm didn't answer. Could even Reb Richardson think he was *that* stupid? The three Rocking X men had just ridden up from Stateline and had known he was here in Kanorado. But it was three against one and he had his own backing stuck somewhere on the infernal prairie, miles away, so he nodded and said, "I'll do that, Reb."

It didn't work. Reb Richardson's eyes went cunning as a coyote's as he said, almost purring, "They told us in

Stateline about you killing old Four Eyes, Longarm."

"Did they? Well, you know how folk gossip in small towns, Reb."

"I do, and you're thinking sneaky thoughts about my cows, ain't you?"

"Not really, Reb. Cows hardly never do anything sneaky. Are we through here? I got some chores to tend, gents."

"You just lied to us about Four Eyes Bronson, damn it."

"Well, fair is fair, Reb. *You* just lied to *me* about where you got them cows in your herd branded with a Double Eight, or a 'U. S.' doctored with an artistic running iron."

Reb Richardson went for his guns. Longarm had expected him to and was already going for his own .44 before he finished the accusation. So it got noisy as hell for a time.

Reb's draw was fast enough, but he made the mistake of standing pat as he fanned his first two rounds through the space where Longarm had been so recently. Then Longarm fired from one knee, off to one side, and as Reb doubled over with a belly full of .44-40, Longarm shifted the other way to blow the side off Spike's face before he could come unstuck.

He might or might not have nailed the one called Noodles. But a shotgun roared behind Longarm and Noodles went down with a gun in his hand and a face made out of strawberry preserves.

Longarm spun on his other knee, smoking sixgun raised, then lowered it with a nod of thanks as he saw Doc Perkins standing there with both barrels of a sawed-off scattergun smoking more. The gambler said, "I told you we was straight, Longarm."

Longarm got to his feet as others from the town came running. He reloaded his .44 as he told Perkins, "I'd say we was more than straight, pard. But would it be impolite to ask how come?"

Doc Perkins shrugged. "Just a sudden impulse, I reckon. I was on my way to the depot, yonder, to see about that train wreck up the line, saw you needed help, and, what the hell."

"You sure saw right, Doc. Do you always pack a scattergun when you check the timetables at the depot?"

Perkins looked sheepish. "All right, I heard you was having a showdown. Call me a sentimental cuss if you like. Or let's just say a gambler fixing to set up shop in Denver can use some friends in high places. Who were we shooting at just now, Longarm?"

"Can't say much about *two* of 'em. One in the middle was Reb Richardson from Texas. So when you get to Denver, keep going, Doc. He's got a brother who talks less and shoots more sudden."

The gambler gulped and said, "Jesus, meeting up with you sure has done wonders for my luck of late. I'd best get my gal and see if we can hire a buckboard and a team. I've heard of the Richardson brothers and I don't reckon we'll wait for no train after all. Could you use a ride, Longarm?"

"Not hardly. I got to stay here for now."

Doc Perkins nodded and moved off through the gathering crowd. Duke Watson elbowed his way through from the other direction, took in the scene near the corral, and whistled softly. Then he asked Longarm if it was over for now.

Longarm said, "It is till my backup or the rest of the Rocking X guns arrive. What happens then will depend a lot on who gets here first. When you write this up, don't put down nothing about me having help. Saves time and paperwork when all the shooting's been done by the law."

"I ain't writing up shit," Duke said. "I'm getting *out* of here! They don't pay me enough to police a town that figures to be blowed sky-high in the near future!"

Chapter 9

By sundown Longarm had wired the home office and knew Billy Vail would have the Texas Rangers cutting off the Rocking X to the south before it could reach its home range again.

The train from Denver arrived just after eight. So Longarm led the two dozen deputies to the saloon after they'd unloaded their mounts at the corral. The deputy in charge was Cutter Mandalian, a dark, husky cuss who'd ridden for the Jingle Bob before joining the Justice Department. As they all bellied up to the bar, Longarm filled Cutter in to date and added, "It looks like we've about wrapped the case poor Pronto Malone was on when he got gunned. Billy Vail was right about the Rocking X stealing government beef, this time. Reb got upset as hell when I mentioned how easy it was to run 'U. S.' to two eights. That's how come they gunned Flynn. Irish must have wondered, too, why they were herding beef from an enemy outfit. Wire I got from

Billy around sunset says Flynn's expected to live, by the way."

Mandalian looked morose and muttered, "It happens that way, sometimes. We come all the way over here for nothing. But what the hell, we're paid by the day, tedious or not. When's the next train back to Denver, pard?"

Longarm said, "Depot says midnight. Why?"

"Why? What in thunder's left for us to do over here on the damned old Ogallala Trail, Longarm? You just said the case is wrapped!"

"No, I didn't. I said the case of the stolen Indian herd was solved. I ain't solved the killing of Pronto Malone yet."

"Hell, wasn't Malone gunned by the Richardsons? *Flynn* sure as hell was!"

Longarm shook his head. "Neither Four Eyes Bronson nor anyone riding for the Rocking X could have murdered Pronto Malone. They hadn't made it this far north from Texas then. Pronto wasn't shot over cows. I'm still working on the motive, so I don't have a decent suspect yet."

Mandalian sipped his beer thoughtfully. "Well, I don't know how me and my boys can help, but we're willing to try," he said. "The boss said you're in charge here, Longarm. What do you want us to do next?"

"You might ride south after the Rocking X," Longarm said. "Your mounts can catch 'em easy, this side of the Texas line, and with Reb and his two top gunslicks out of the picture, they shouldn't give you much of a fight."

"I ain't worried about a fight with anybody. But you just said you had the Texas Rangers heading 'em off, Longarm."

"I know. And if the stolen Indian beef outpaces you, the Rangers will nail 'em sure. Meanwhile, a deputy U. S. marshal was murdered while investigating said stolen beef. So whose beef *is* it, Cutter, the Rangers' or the Justice Department's?"

Mandalian said, "Ours. We owe it to old Pronto, even if he was an idjet about to get fired."

Longarm sighed. "You heard, huh?"

Mandalian said, "It wasn't hard to hear. The attorney general was yelling his fool head off when they had to let that counterfeiting gal go free. In a way it's just as well old Pronto got kilt on the job. This way his widow woman will get his pension. They'd have drummed him outten the service in disgrace had he lived long enough."

Longarm shrugged and said, "Well, he did, and we owe it to his widow woman, at least, to see his last case wrapped by his pards. But while we're on the subject of the other woman in Pronto's life, was she a real counterfeiter or just passing queer? I've a reason for asking."

"Nobody will ever know now," Mandalian said. "Like I said, she got off scot free and knows she's being watched. She didn't have no counterfeiting plates on her or in her rooms when she was arrested. But from the way both Treasury and the attorney general carried on, they must have thought she was sort of important. I don't know much about the case. Only seen her once, in the federal building. She was some looker, but Pronto was still an idjet to mess with her, invited or otherwise."

He finished his beer and called out, "Vamanos, muchachos! We got us some riding to do, unless you boys are scared of cow thieves!"

Somebody yelled, "Powder River and let her buck!" and the whole crew left Longarm alone to go chasing the Rocking X.

Longarm started to order another. Then he looked at the wall clock again and decided he'd see if old Fanny had kept his supper warm. Now that things figured to stay quiet for a time, he was already regretting his warning to her about his tumbleweed ways.

They hadn't put in streetlights yet, or even a real street, so as Longarm headed down to Fanny's end of the bitty town the only illumination came from the few lit windows on either side. It was even darker near the gunsmith shop, of course. The front of Fanny's shop was dark and the only light that way came from the lamp over the Western Union's all-night office.

He decided it would be more sensible to go around to Fanny's rear entrance and, if that was dark, too, forget it. Gals had the right to change their minds.

The killer following him in the dark must not have expected him to suddenly cut to one side. He'd been aiming at Longarm's head, outlined by the Western Union lamp. So when he fired, Longarm's head just wasn't there anymore.

Even so, it was close enough. A pellet of number nine buck ticked the brim of Longarm's Stetson as the big deputy spun and drew, crouched low in the dark, and then, when the shotgun blazed a second time, aimed wild, Longarm aimed better at the flash and heard both the shotgun and its owner thudding to the dust in the dark. He fired at the biggest thud, for luck, and when it didn't even groan, moved in for a better look.

It was Doc Perkins. Longarm wasn't too surprised, once he studied on it. He kicked the cadaver with a boot tip and said, "So you *was* aiming at my back when you blew old Noodles away, eh? You sure shoots awful for a man with such a mean disposition, Doc."

Doc Perkins didn't answer. That didn't surprise Longarm either. He heard running footsteps and a door behind him opened with a little tinkle. "Get back inside, Miss Fanny," he said. "I'll tell you about it later, after I explains it to the whole infernal town!"

She ran out to him, dressed modestly but still sort of

scandalous in a house robe, and sobbed, "Oh, Custis! I knew it had to be you when I heard that .44-40 and I was so afraid for you!"

He said he'd been scared a mite, himself. Then Duke Watson ran up to them and struck a match to see who had been shot. "Damn it, Longarm, I was hoping this would be Tex Richardson!" he said.

Longarm said, "Sorry. Tex ain't even had time to have heard about his brother yet. This here's a gambling man I took at poker this afternoon. As you can see, he was a poor loser. Dumb as hell, too. He went after me twice in the same way. Mayhaps he figured his aim might improve if he just kept trying. Could you handle the paperwork on this one, too, Duke? I got some chores as need tending, now."

Duke Watson muttered something mean about Longarm's ancestry and called out to a couple of town deputies for help with the remains. As Longarm reholstered his reloaded gun Fanny took him by the arm and murmured, "Let's get you inside before you can get in any more trouble!"

He said, "I'm already in trouble, Miss Fanny. But you can leave your rear door open to me, if you've still a mind to. I got to go to yonder telegraph office first."

She let him go and ducked inside. Longarm found a new Western Union clerk on duty. He picked up a pencil and a blank to bring the office up to date with a few words as he asked the telegraph clerk, "Has anybody wired anything about me, anywheres, recent? I've got a reason for asking."

The clerk said, "Western Union messages are privileged information, sir."

"I ain't no sir," Longarm said. "I'm a deputy U. S. marshal and your wires run over lots of U. S. open range. So would you like to rephrase that answer more sensible, friend?"

"Well, I'm not supposed to divulge such matters, but,

since you put it so delicately, a lady was in here earlier this evening, and she did mention your name in passing when she wired Waco, Texas."

"Did she wire anyone named Richardson? And what did she say about me in her infernal wire?"

"Well, she did tell a certain party his brother was dead, and how come. You're going to get me in trouble, reading other people's telegrams this way."

"You've told me all I needed to know, and I thank you. What did this mysterious she-male look like?"

"I thought you said that was all you needed to know."

"Damn it—"

"All right, all right, she was a little blond gal, dressed fancy but sort of shabby, like she'd been on the road a spell in a once-new maroon dress. Fake cotton velvet, I think. She sent the wire collect and never left a name or return address."

Longarm nodded and said, "All right, we won't cut your poles down after all. Should she come in again, make sure you don't tell her what you just told me, hear? I like to surprise folk. Just send any wire she wants you to send and make sure you keep a copy for me."

"That's not allowed, sir."

"Sparks . . ."

"Yes, sir. Just don't ever tell the company on me."

Longarm smiled thinly and left for Fanny's. She insisted on feeding him coffee and cake as she made him tell her all about the shooting out front. When he'd finished, Fanny asked, "Doesn't that mean you got the man who shotgunned your fellow deputy, Custis?"

Longarm grimaced. "I'm still studying on that. Doc could have lied about never having been in Stateline. My office will check that angle out. Meanwhile his bitty blond gal pal is wandering about out there, somewhere, mad as hell at me. I hope she got most of the spite out of her system by wiring Reb Richardson's brother the glad tidings. She wired him before old Doc come after me again, so she might have been hoping to get me killed before Doc could try for me again. She must have noticed he had a surly disposition, poor thing."

The bigger gal nearer to hand said, "Brrr! She could be stalking you this very minute and you don't even know what she looks like!"

He said, "Yeah, even if she has another dress, it's hard to spot a she-male from a he-male in the dark. I'm hoping she'll be smart enough to catch the midnight train."

"Don't you want to arrest her, Custis?"

"Sure, but I don't want to gun a woman, and there's no way I can get near her now without having to. It's smarter just to let her light out. If she ain't here in town come morning when it'll be easier to tell, I'll wire Denver and they can pick her up, less noisy. How far can a strange blonde in a velvet dress get in a strange town, flat busted? It was my busting her and Doc so flat as caused all the ill-will betwixt us, see?"

"My, you *do* think ahead, don't you? I suppose you might think ahead and get the wrong idea if I was to suggest you stay here for the night and let that wild, wicked woman search for you in vain."

He grinned at her. "I hardly ever get wrong ideas unless I'm invited to. What sort of ideas do you want me to have, Miss Fanny?"

She laughed and said, "There's no point in fencing with a mind reader. Why don't we just talk about our future plans in bed, like sensible adults?"

He stood up and trimmed the lamp. Fanny beat him into the nearby four-poster unfairly, not having as much to take off. But he forgave her when he finished shucking and groped his way into her bed, and her.

She hissed in pleasure as he entered her and reclined on her considerable charms. He was pleased, too, for she was nice and tight for such a big gal. As he started loping in the saddle Fanny sighed and said, "Oh, heavenly, but I suppose you're just being nice to a big old cow like me, aren't you?"

He said, "Honey, if cows was built anything like you, few cowboys would ever come to town! I like the way you're put together fine. It's nice to kiss a gal without having to scrootch all up as you're screwing her."

She gasped, "Oh, I wish you wouldn't put it so crudely, dear. I prefer to think of this as, well, adultery or some such refined word."

He laughed. "Well, we're surely screwing adult, but to qualify as adultery, one of us at least is supposed to be married up with someone else."

She didn't answer as he pounded harder. He feared he might have said something wrong. But when she wrapped her big long legs around him and dug her nails into his bare back, he figured she was just one of them quiet screwing gals. So he shut up and just treated her right until they climaxed together. As Fanny lay in his arms, pulsing warmly, she recovered from whatever was making her so thought-some and said with an earthy laugh, "You're right, of course. It's silly to pretend delicacy. Let's just *do* it, hot and dirty. I'll confess I'm a little out of practice, dear, but I've always been a really wild slut, once I've gotten good and hot!"

"Are you hot now, Miss Fanny?"

"You know I am!"

He hooked one of her knees over each of his own elbows to spread her high and wide, but it didn't seem to scare her much. She moved her long legs even higher, hooked her

108

bare toes into the bed rails above their heads, and damned near bucked him out of bed as she moved her big hips wild as hell. She said it made her feel helpless, and he didn't argue. He was sure glad she didn't want to have a bare-knuckles fight with him to see who was boss.

She moaned in pleasure and said, "Oh, I felt that! Don't stop! Please don't stop! For God's sake don't..."

He figured they could both use a rest, for now. So he dismounted, found the shirt he'd dropped on the floor by the bed, and climbed in with her sensible to cuddle and smoke. She asked, "Are you through already? We've barely gotten to know one another."

He chuckled. "It lasts longer if you stop for breath now and again, honey. Do you smoke, by the way?"

She said, "No, thanks. I only have one real vice. Can you guess what it is, darling?"

It hardly called for guesswork as he felt her unbound hair sweeping down across his bare belly. He lit his cheroot, admiring the view of all that naked she-male flesh on its hands and knees, and said, "When you told me you was a wild woman in bed, you surely wasn't fibbing!"

Fanny didn't answer. She couldn't, with her mouth full.

Longarm gasped with pleased surprise as her pursed wet lips slid up and down his semi-sated shaft with a skill few fancy gals might have managed. He didn't ask her where she'd learned to suck like that. She'd said her old man was dead, the poor bastard.

His semi-erection didn't last as long as his cheroot. So he snuffed it out and groaned, "Hey, waste not, want not, Fanny! Let's do it right, lest I do something shocking in your pretty face!"

She mumbled, with her mouth filled, *"Do* it! Shoot in your little love slave's mouth!"

He knew he was fixing to shoot it somewhere, soon. So he groped for her unused loving parts in the dark and proceeded to return the favor with his fingers. She must have liked it, from the way she was biting down on his fingers.

His distraction, added to the earlier thrills of her considerable flesh, held Longarm's orgasm back enough so she came again first, damned near breaking his knuckles as she swallowed him to the roots and rubbed her nose against his nuts like a lovesick Eskimo as he climaxed in her tight throat and nearly fainted.

She sat up, saying, "Oh, yum yum yum. Let me get on top, now."

He didn't have much to say about it, it would seem. And she used her long limbs to further advantage that way, too. In the dark he gasped, "How in thunder are you moving it like that, honey?"

Fanny laughed and answered, "I have one foot on the floor. Do you like it this way?"

"Honey, I'd like it hanging upside down like a bat with you. But ain't it my turn to do the work?"

She said she knew a way they could both move freely. So he said he was game and she hauled him out of bed with her surprising strength and said, "Let's dance. I'll lead."

He started to tell her it wouldn't work so good standing up. For, like most men, he'd tried it in his day and found his legs were just too long. But as he grabbed a bedpost to steady them Fanny took his shaft in hand, stood on tiptoe to guide it in, and he found out it did work when the gal's legs were as long as his.

She was built a mite shorter than him, above the crotch, so when he bent his head to kiss her upturned face in the dark Fanny giggled and told him she'd wanted him to do this to her the first time he'd kissed her that afternoon. This didn't surprise him at all. But it was sort of confusing, albeit nice, when she hooked one long leg up over the arm he was holding the bedpost by, to bump and grind against him in a standing split.

It was tiring as well as interesting, and it wasn't as if they'd just started. So he suggested they get back into a more relaxed position. She said that was fine with her, turned around, and bent over to grab her own ankles as she leaned back against him, stiff-legged and him still standing. He grabbed a big hip in each hand and pulled her on and off like a boot filled with marshmallow until she sobbed, fell off him to the floor, and pleaded, "More, more!"

He dropped down on her to finish, but it sure felt like rough loving with her tailbone braced on the bare planks and his knees picking up splinters while they both went crazy for a spell. When they'd finished that way, Fanny said she loved the helpless feeling as he crushed her with his bigger body. He was glad it made her feel good, but he doubted she was all that helpless.

The pounding on the floor seemed to have simmered her down some, though, for before he finished his second smoke, she was snoring soft as a contented kitten with her face buried against his chest. He put out the smoke and went to sleep himself, while he had the chance.

For some reason they both slept soundly till a rooster crowed at the rising sun, outside. Fanny sat up in bed, looking sort of confused as well as drowsy. Then she gasped, "Oh, it's daylight and we're both stark naked!"

He said, "I noticed," as he hauled her down for a morning kiss. She kissed back passionately, but then she said, "I'm so embarrassed. Even my husband never saw me naked in the light. I should have put my robe back on before I fell asleep, damn it."

He asked, "What for? It'd only have to come off again. It's too early to get up, honey, but I sure am wide awake right now."

She looked down and gasped, "Oh, dear, I can see you are! Doesn't it embarrass you to be exposed like that, Custis?"

"Why should it? Most men have peckers and I suspicion most women knows we has."

She giggled, told him he was awful, and that she was sure she was too big and fat for him. He said, "The only thing getting big and fat around here's anxious to get back inside your pretty little hide, honey. So lay back right and let's get to it."

"Oh, I couldn't in broad daylight," she insisted coyly.

But she was wrong. For once they'd gotten started again she forgot her shyness and even allowed this was a new and delightfully dirty way to start the day.

When they'd finished, he said he had to study on the day ahead of them, too. She asked how long he'd be able to stay in town. He said, "Won't know till I check at the Western Union. I sure hope that gambling man's little blonde left town last night."

"The poor thing didn't know what she was missing. Who'd ever want to shoot you, when you shoot so good in every way?"

He said some gals weren't as friendly as her, so she laid him again and then she said it was time to fix some breakfast. She wanted to do so with her robe on. But he talked her out of it and she seemed to get a kick out of puttering about with her stove and fixings in no more than an apron, lest she spill grease on her body. But he got her to take it off, giggling, as they ate breakfast on the bed together. They had each other for dessert, but by now they both knew they'd gotten past passion into just plain showing off. So when Longarm said he had to go, she didn't argue, but asked

112

when and if she'd see him again.

He said he'd surely be back if there was any way at all he could stay in town a spell. She sighed and said, "I hope so. I confess I've never been so satisfied before with any man. As you might have guessed, it takes a lot of man to satisfy me."

He said something about understanding the feelings of a warm-natured widow woman. Then, catching the look on her face, he frowned. "You did tell me you was a widow woman, didn't you, Fanny?" he asked.

Her face turned red as she looked away. "Please don't spoil it, Custis. You can see I'm alone here, can't you?"

"Yeah, thank God, but let's get down to brass tacks, girl. Are you a widow woman or ain't you?"

She covered her face with her hands and blurted, "He's not here *now*, is he? Why do you have to be so nosy? I might have fibbed a little, but you enjoyed it as much as me and, anyway, a woman like me has feelings no one man can satisfy."

Longarm swung his naked legs off the bed and started getting dressed as Fanny insisted, "He won't be back for at least two weeks. You don't have to worry about us getting caught, darling!"

He didn't answer, he just kept dressing. When he stood to stomp his boots on, Fanny sighed. "I told you I was a slut, dear. You didn't seem to mind at the time," she said ruefully.

He put on his hat and headed for the door. She cried out, "Wait, we have to talk! You have to give me a chance to explain!"

He opened the door, stepped out, and closed it softly behind him as she wailed something spiteful inside. He walked off shaking his head with disgust—not with the cheating wife back there, but at himself for being such a fool. That made two gals in a row he'd allowed to slicker him. At the rate he was going, he'd wind up as bad as old Pronto Malone.

Then he frowned thoughtfully and went to the Western Union to find out if a big old gal with big old feet had been in Stateside recent.

Chapter 10

By noon Longarm had established that nobody in Stateside recalled a big woman, knowledgeable about guns, in town at the time of Pronto Malone's death by gunfire. He couldn't ask about Fanny's possibly possessive husband, since he didn't know what the poor bastard looked like. Nobody in Kanorado could say for certain if a blonde in maroon velvet had left town or not. So, small as the town was, he wired Vail he meant to ride on up the line. He wasn't getting anywhere with Pronto's killing in Kanorado. But it was unsettling to consider a strange man and a gal, who might own another dress, both out to kill him at the same time. He didn't wire Vail what he expected to find at the next trail town north. He didn't know. He only knew it was dumb to stay in Kanorado. So he got his saddle and possibles from the whorehouse, thanking the ladies kindly for an offer he had to refuse, and saddled up to ride north.

It was tedious as hell. The prairie was bone dry now even in the draws, and as thirsty to look out across as the real sea some called the Sea of Grass.

He suppered out of cold cans at sundown, letting his mount rest and graze some, then, as the moon rose, rode on, hoping to make the next wide spot in the Ogallala Trail by midnight.

He'd ridden less than an hour when he noticed he had company on the Ogallala Trail. Hoofbeats were dogging him at a discreet distance. The moon was over Kansas. So Longarm rode west into Colorado a ways, reined in, and hauled his saddle gun out of its boot to dismount and see what happened next.

Then he laughed. A riderless horse was outlined by the moonlight as it advanced hesitant as a friendly but wary pup, nickering to Longarm's mount. Longarm swung himself back up into the saddle and the critter spooked off a ways, but stopped and nickered again.

Longarm shoved the Winchester back in its boot as he asked the stranger, "Didn't your owner know you were coming into heat, ma'am? I can see you run off for a wild and wicked night on the prairie. But you come to the wrong place. This here's a gelding, and I've sworn off females for good!"

The mare twirled around and presented her rump to them, saying something dirty in Horse. Longarm laughed again and steadied his own mount, telling it, "That's life, pard. She's too fat for me and you just ain't got the balls."

Then he stiffened and fell silent as the night echoed to yet another set of hoofbeats, coming from the north lickey-split. Someone was in one hell of a hurry over there on the trail. He couldn't be chasing anyone. So unless he was just a natural speed demon, somebody could be chasing him.

Longarm wasn't outlined by the moon. The strange rider was. So he got a fair look at him in passing and the first

116

thing he noticed was that it was a she. It was a gal heading south with her long hair streaming north. The mare in heat nickered and ran after the new and possibly hornier mount. The gal heard and whipped her lathered mount into a faster run. Longarm told his own mount, "We'd best stand pat here till we see if anyone but that fool runaway's really after the lady."

Nobody was. At least, nobody else came down the trail for a good twenty minutes or more. So Longarm decided that if anyone had ever been chasing the gal, she'd lost them in the dark. He shrugged and said, "Likely a lovers' quarrel. No posse would give up so easy. Let's move on up the trail, pard."

He'd been planning on arriving at midnight, but it was more like one A. M. when he rode into the mushroom town of Coldwater, Colorado—or Kansas, depending on which side of the main street you might be on. The little town was brightly lit and noisy for this late, with no trail herd in evidence. It looked like the local citizens were expecting at least a circus to come to town.

Longarm reined in by yet another Last Chance Saloon, tethered his mount, and stepped through the batwings to get a beer and his bearings. The place was crowded, the piano was loud, and nobody paid Longarm any mind as he bellied up to the bar and said he'd drink anything wet but preferred needled beer. The jovial barkeep slid a schooner across the mahogany and said, "You gotta pay for that'n, but ever' third one's on the house. You ride in to attend the hanging, stranger?"

Longarm put a cartwheel on the bar and replied, "Just passing through. Didn't know you were hanging anyone. What's the story?"

The cowhand next to Longarm laughed. "The usual one.

They caught them a hoss thief red-handed. Or mayhaps I should say red-rumped, for the idjet rode his purloined hoss right into the very town he stole it from. Ain't that a joke?"

Longarm nodded. "I've met a few dumb horse thieves in my day. But are all these folks here just to see a horse thief do the rope dance?"

"Sure. The opera house ain't built yet. Don't even have a regular gallows. But the feed store says we can use their loading crane so's everyone can get a good look at the idjet as he's heisted."

Longarm shrugged and swallowed needled beer until he couldn't taste prairie dust any more. He couldn't help feeling a mite sorry for the object of the town's festive mood. The federal government didn't hang horse thieves, but the State of Colorado did, and he knew better than to ask which side of the street the jailhouse was on.

He had more important worries than the fate of a careless petty crook. He asked the friendly locals if there was a Western Union office handy. The cowhand who'd ridden in to attend the morning necktie party looked blank. The barkeep said Coldwater had neither a railroad nor a telegraph line as yet. Longarm asked how long ago the Double Eight had been through. The barkeep said they were about a day ahead of him, if he hurried.

Longarm said he wasn't trying to catch up with the Double Eight. He saw no reason to say who he was or what his business in town might be just yet. For one thing, he wasn't sure. It just beat hanging about Kanorado until a jealous husband or a spiteful woman pegged a shot at him.

He'd just finished his first schooner and was debating with himself about ordering a second or finding out about the hotel situation here in Coldwater when a little townee sidled up to him and whispered, "There's a lady as would like a word with you, Mr. Long."

Longarm picked up his change and followed the townee, opening his frock coat to clear his gun, just in case. But when he spied the gal by the piano he smiled back at her, albeit a mite puzzled. Her face was more than familiar. Her hair was red, blond, or black, depending on her mood. Tonight it was red again, to match her too-short Dolly Varden dress of shiny silk. As the townee peeled off to rejoin the festivities in the crowded saloon, Longarm said, "Howdy, Miss Ruby. I'm sort of surprised to meet up with you here. Last time we bumped noses you told me you'd reformed."

Ruby laughed, low and husky. "We bumped more than noses, as I recalls with pleasure, and I *has* reformed. I own this place. I don't service the customers myself, present company excepted. What are you doing here in Coldwater, Custis? If she's prettier than me I'll snatch her bald-headed."

Longarm laughed. "I've swore off womankind, present company excepted, Miss Ruby. I ain't sure *what* in thunder I'm doing here, as a matter of fact, but a man has to be somewhere and I hates to go home empty-handed. They sent me to find the one as shot Pronto Malone. You remember him?"

The temporary redhead wrinkled her pert nose and replied, "Not fondly. I heard about him getting kilt down in Stateline. Good riddance to a plague on womankind, if you ask me!"

"Old Pronto had his faults, I'll allow, but it's still unlawful to shotgun a lawman on duty."

"If you say so, lover man. Do you expect to meet up with his killer here in my place? If you do, I'd best get the sawdust ready."

He laughed wryly and assured her, "To tell the truth, the trail's as cold as a banker's heart, Miss Ruby. I've run out of leads entire. But, like I said, I got to keep sniffing about at least until my Uncle Billy says I can come home."

Ruby dimpled. "Speaking of sniffing around, I got to watch the house and my new barkeep for a spell. But if you'd like to wait upstairs in my chambers, we can lie down to talk about old times in the cold gray light, after the hanging. Things should go dead in town once he is."

Longarm said, "I thank you kindly for the invite, but I got a tired mount out front as needs food and shelter, too."

"Put it in my stable out back. What's the matter, Custis? You look sort of undecided. Ain't we pals no more?"

He grinned down at her. They'd been more than pals in the past and it felt good to meet up with a woman he could trust. He'd ridden out of Kanorado convinced he never wanted to kiss another of the treacherous critters, but that had been a spell back, and the long ride north had restored his appetite some. He said, "Hold the thought. Got to put my mount to bed first."

He went out front, untethered his mount, and led it around to Ruby's stable. He unsaddled it, rubbed it down with dry sacking, and put it in a stall with some water and oats he found handy. Then he went back to see if Ruby still admired him.

She brightened when she saw him really coming back. "Damn, I wish it was morning. I don't know how in hell I'm to hold out till the hanging. You reckon I could trust my new help for fifteen minutes?"

He chuckled and said, "Honey, you know me and I know you. Once we got your stays off, you'd never in this world settle for a quarter of an hour in paradise. We just got to be patient. What time are they hanging the poor bastard?"

"Sunrise. That won't be for hours, damn it! Why in hell did he have to ride back to town on the very horse he stole? I'll allow it's good for business, but, damn it, I'm really gushing for you bad. You know I never fools with local talent, so it's been ages since I last got laid. Even longer since I had someone like *you,* to do it *right!*"

Her bawdy words were having a vexing effect on his own delicate feelings, now that he'd found a trustworthy gal he remembered as one hell of a lay. To change the subject, he said, "Let's talk about the hanging. I don't suppose a judge and jury was involved?"

Ruby shrugged. "Our elected mayor is our acting judge. It was a fair enough trial. The stupid son of a bitch checked into the boarding house down the street with a Mexican gal and the horses he'd stole on the very same block."

Longarm asked Ruby, "Would this accused horse thief be a prissy-dressed dude hailing from Virginia?"

Ruby shrugged again. "Don't know where he hailed from, but he was a snappy dresser, all right. The Mex gal got away in the confusion, but it don't matter. She was riding a paint nobody around here was missing. They got the rascal as matters and . . . Where you going, honey lamb?"

Longarm called back, "Got to see me a town marshal about a suspect. I'll be back directly."

He pushed his way out to the street, asked directions to the local lockup, and went there. He found a couple of deputies seated on the steps with shotguns. But when he told them who he was and that he hadn't come to lynch their prisoner early they let him go on in.

The town marshal got up from behind his desk to greet Longarm, looking pleased with himself and the world, as well he should have, with that nice new silver-mounted ivory-gripped sixgun riding in his old worn holster. Longarm showed him his federal badge and asked if he could talk to the prisoner. So the town marshal led him back to the cellblock where the con man he'd met in Fanny's gunsmith shop was sitting morosely on a cot.

As Longarm stepped up to the bars the prisoner looked up, swore, and said, "Oh, hell, I thought everything that could go wrong had already done so. I thought I'd gotten away from you, Longarm."

Longarm said, "I see Estralita told you who I was. She's still running loose, if it's any comfort to you. She'll likely do better as a hotel maid again. You ought to be ashamed of yourself."

The prisoner shrugged. "I am. Did they tell you what a stupid stunt I pulled in this town?"

"They didn't even tell me your name, so let's start with that."

"Oh, I thought that two-faced Mex gal might have told you. I'm Montjoy Cavendish, from Fairfax County, Virginia."

Longarm doubted that, but he let it go. He said, "Well, Monty, you sure made a hell of a mistake, riding that horse you stole back to its home town. Didn't anybody ever tell you Colorado takes a dim view about stealing horses? They only puts you in prison for stealing cows, unless the cowhand catches you first, of course. But men has died stranded in dry country without a mount, so they passed some serious laws on the subject."

Cavendish protested, "Damn it, I never stole any horse. I bought it in Stateline, fair and square. My own mount had gone lame and—"

"Spare me the old, sad, too-familiar story, Monty," Longarm cut in. "I just come to see if you could clear up some details about the day Pronto Malone got gunned in Stateline, seeing as you was there at the time."

Cavendish sighed, buried his face in his hands, and sobbed, "Oh, hell, what's the use. You got me, Longarm."

Longarm frowned and asked, "Got you for what? Stealing horses ain't a federal crime, you idjet."

"Don't play cat and mouse with me, you bastard. I know your rep. You never rode all this way after me without a reason, and what other reason would there be?"

Longarm studied the man behind the bars a long hard time before he nodded and said, "Yeah, a man who'd just gunned a federal officer would have reasons for leaving town on the first horse handy. That makes more sense than you riding up here with a mount stole from Coldwater just to return it to its owner."

Cavendish stood up, came over to the bars pale-faced, and said, "Listen, Longarm, it wasn't murder. It was a fair fight. How was I to know the man was a federal officer when he called me out for a fight?"

"Tell me about it," said Longarm flatly.

Cavendish said, "It was over a woman. Not the Mex gal. A fair-headed white gal Malone was sparking, only I didn't know it. I didn't do nothing wrong to the gal. I just invited her up to my hotel room to, well, look at my stamp collection or something. Malone walked in on us as we were sort of flirting, and you know the rest."

Longarm said, "No, I don't. Pronto was stupid about women, but not about guns. You never in this world took Pronto Malone in a fair fight, even with a scattergun!"

Cavendish looked down at the gritty cement floor and said sheepishly, "All right, mayhaps I had a little edge. He told me he was going for a stroll and that if I was still in town when he got back, he'd kill me. So, all right, I laid for him between the buildings with my saddle gun and when he passed, I stepped out, called his name, and fired as he turned. But, hell, Longarm, he was a professional gunslick. I had to have *some* edge, didn't I?"

Longarm didn't answer as he stared poker-faced at the prisoner.

Cavendish licked his lips and said, "It was a fair fight,

I swear to God. You gotta believe me."

Longarm said, "A man standing as close to the gates of hell as you ought to go easy on taking the name of the Lord in vain. It ain't for me to say what a judge and jury might or might not believe. But, for all his faults, Pronto Malone didn't read Ned Buntline's western romances serious enough to follow such fool advice as setting up an appointment for a gunfight."

"It was his notion, not mine—I swear!"

"Sure it was. I've often thought how smart it would be for me to tell a man with a gun ahead of time where I'd be expecting him to meet me for a fair fight. The trouble is, I've never figured out what was to prevent him from getting there a mite early, to fire at me from cover as I come strolling down the street!"

Cavendish looked sheepish. "Mayhaps he wasn't as smart as you, Longarm," was all he said.

Longarm shrugged. "Like I said, it's for the judge and jury to decide. Don't go 'way. I'll be back directly."

He went back out to the office and told the town marshal, "I'm sorry, pard, but I fear I has to take your prisoner back to Denver with me to stand trial on a federal rap."

The town law said, "No, you ain't. We got a German band coming and a root beer stand already set up. You can have the remains after we get done hanging the hoss thief, though. Saves the town the expense of a funeral."

Longarm said, "You don't understand. Federal law has jurisdiction over local. The rascal just confessed, sort of, to the cold-blooded murder of a federal officer!"

The town law shook his head. *"You're* the one who don't understand, Longarm. We seen him first. I couldn't turn him over to you if I wanted to, which I don't, this being an election year. Everyone for miles around has rid in to see a hanging in the morning, and if they don't see one they're likely to get testy as hell. There's a couple of hundred guns betwixt you and Denver, Longarm. So why don't you just act sensible and enjoy the German band with ever'one else in the morning? It ain't like the son of a bitch ain't going to *pay* for his erring ways, you know."

"Are you telling the U. S. government to go to hell, friend?"

"I sure am. You can write a letter to your congressman if you don't admire our manners here in Coldwater. But we're still hanging the son of a bitch, legal and proper."

Longarm frowned. "Bullshit! Cavendish is a federal prisoner, as of the moment he confessed to a federal crime."

The town marshal grinned up at him and said, "I'll tell you what, Longarm. You show me a writ from a superior court ordering me to turn the prisoner over to you, and I'll consider it real hard."

"Oh, thanks a lot! How in thunder am I to contact a federal judge betwixt here and the cold, gray dawn? You don't even have a telegraph in your infernal bitty trail town!"

"That's *your* problem, Longarm. *My* problem is showing the folks the show they rid in to see. Just simmer down and study on it some, and you'll see I'm acting within the law—federal, state, and local."

Longarm didn't argue the matter further. He'd had the same discussion in the past with other big frogs in little puddles. He shrugged and said, "Well, at least I tried. I thanks you for your time and, seeing there's nothing more I can do here, I may as well head home."

"Ain't you staying for the hanging, Longarm?"

"What for? Once you've seen one hanging you've seen 'em all."

He didn't check his watch until he'd left the jailhouse

and was entering Ruby's Last Chance again. His watch told him he'd better hurry up. He found Ruby in the back of the crowd and said, "I got a hell of a problem, honey. Let's go out back to the stable and talk about it."

She frowned uncertainly and asked, "In the stable? I ain't done it in a stable since I was twelve. But, all right—*I* got a hell of a problem, too."

She took his hand to lead him out the back way. As they entered the side door of her stable, a couple of the critters inside whinnied. Ruby laughed. "Come on, the ladder to the hay loft's this way."

He stopped her and said, "Hold on, Miss Ruby. You know I'd like to lay you, but I ain't got time."

"You ain't? Then what in the hell am I doing out here in the dark with you, honey-hoss?"

He said, "The mount I rid up here aboard is too jaded for a serious discussion of speed. So I'll need two good mounts and an extra saddle. I mean, right now, hear?"

"Oh, is somebody here in Coldwater after you, Custis?"

"Not yet, but they will be. I'll leave my livery mount here with you. Then I'll leave your two in the corral down in Kanorado. You can send someone aboard my brute, once he's rested, and ship him to Denver on the train. Then he can ride one of yourn and lead the other back. I'll naturally leave him the borrowed saddle and..."

"Never mind all that," Ruby said. "Who's after you and how serious? I've got some good men working for me, if you needs a backup, Custis."

It was tempting, but he shook his head and said, "No thanks. Don't want no more killing, if it can be avoided. I reckon it can, if you've a couple of good horses handy, Miss Ruby."

"Well, the fastest critters I own are the matched thoroughbreds I drives, and they ain't been drove, recent."

He frowned. "Have said carriage horses been saddle broke, Miss Ruby?"

She shrugged and replied, "How should I know? I'm a lady, not a cowboy. I rides about proper, in my right expensive buggy. Them thoroughbreds cost me a bundle, too. They're high-stepping strutters as can go like the wind."

He considered. "Well, no cow pony foaled of mortal mare is about to overtake a thoroughbred with a good lead on it. Such big, dumb horses seldom buck enough to matter. So I'll have to chance it. What about the extra saddle?"

"There's saddles galore in the tackroom, yonder. But afore you mounts horse one of mine, how's about mounting me, first?"

He started to tell her there wasn't time. But she was already on her knees in front of him, opening his fly, and he knew the quickest way to make her let him go would be to make her come. So he laughed and said, "I don't need a French lesson for inspiration, honey. Let's get up that fool ladder to do it right!"

He goosed her, going up the ladder after her, and Ruby laughed and dove headfirst into the hay above as he followed, shedding his hat, coat, and guns. Ruby didn't waste time undressing, either. She lay back in the hay, hoisted her Dolly Varden up around her corseted waist, and spread her legs wide in what would have been a shocking display of bawdy behavior, had there been more light. As it was, he could see she'd worn no pantaloons under her skirts and her black silk stockings were gartered just above her knees. So he dropped his own pants and dropped down on her to renew their old friendship before the infernal sun could come up.

She gasped, "Jesus! Let a lady warm up a mite before

127

you try to shove it out her mouth, you horny rascal!"

But the nice thing about exploring places you'd been before was that you knew what you were doing and didn't have to be shy. Old Ruby always complained about his pecker being too big for her, but he knew she was just being complimentful. So he screwed her hard and fast, the way he knew she liked it, even though she kept whimpering about him abusing her. She moved her hips like a skilled whore, but it was true she'd given up that trade before he'd even laid her the first time. So the end result was true romance with professional skill, and it sure felt wild.

She must have liked what she was doing, too. She gasped, "Deeper, get it *deeper*, damn it, I'm almost there!"

He reached down to grab her silk-sheathed legs, hauled them up on either side, then got a hand under each of her knees to flatten them in the hay on either side of her head as he raised his body with his weight on his hands and screwed her with a spiral motion, clockwise, as she gyrated her hot love pit counterclockwise. The results were explosive. Ruby gasped, "Powder River and let her buck! I don't know if I'm coming or dying, but I'll kill you if you stop!"

He had to, once he'd come in her twice. She said she forgave him, since she was three climaxes ahead of him. So they went down the ladder and she helped him saddle her thoroughbreds. She begged him for a wall job against a stall before he left, but he told her not to be silly.

Chapter 11

It was still dark, but Longarm knew it wouldn't be much longer as he led the two thoroughbreds on foot around to the back of the jailhouse. As he'd hoped, the rear of the cinder-block building wasn't guarded because, as he'd seen inside, there was neither a back door nor one barred window in the featureless blank walls behind the front office. The stoutly built town lockup did have internal plumbing, however. There was a sewer gas pipe sticking out through the flat roof near one corner. Longarm tethered the mounts to a drain pipe running down the wall, took the throw-rope from the stock saddle he'd borrowed from Ruby, and shook out a community loop. The moon was down now, but the lights from the main drag on the far side of the building outlined the roof vent well enough. So he swung the rope a couple of times as he gauged the distance and roped it with his first throw.

He hauled himself up to the tarpaper-covered roof, crawled to the stretch above the only prisoner's cell as he recoiled the rope, then quietly went to work on the tarpaper with his pocketknife.

As he'd hoped, there was only one layer of pine planking under the waterproof tarpaper. The weak spot in the jailhouse architect's plans was that he'd naturally never expected the place to hold anyone twelve feet tall. So he hadn't worried about anyone punching a hole in the roof from below. It was a lot easier, working from the top.

Longarm silently eased some nails loose with the screwdriver blade of his knife, pried two planks up out of the way, and hissed down at Cavendish in the cell below. The prisoner jumped half out of his skin, looked up, and gasped, "What the hell?" But he was smart enough to gasp it softly.

Longarm dropped the loop end of the rope down into the cell as he whispered, "There's two ways you can choose, Cavendish. You can stay there and hang in less'n two hours, or you can grab hold and take your chances with a federal grand jury you might not go before for at least a week."

Cavendish grabbed the rope. Longarm had figured he might. So he stood up, braced his heels, and hauled the smaller man up and out of jail. Then he said, "Sit down. Don't make any sudden moves unless you aim to die here and now."

Cavendish did as he was told. Longarm put the planking back in place. The more time they spent studying on how Cavendish had gotten out, the more time Longarm had to get him further off before they saddled up.

His chore finished, Longarm handcuffed Cavendish, sat him in the noose, and lowered him to the ground near the horses. There was nobody to lower Longarm, if he meant to keep the rope. He had to return it to Ruby, in time. So he just jumped down. It didn't hurt much.

He picked himself up from the dust, boosted Cavendish

aboard a tethered horse, quickly recoiled the rope and refastened it to his prisoner's stock saddle, then untethered both brutes, mounted the one saddled with his McClellan and possibles, and murmured, "Let's move out at a walk, at first."

Cavendish didn't argue as he held his own reins in his cuffed hands. Once they were clear a quarter mile, Longarm said, "Now let's ride. Hang on to the horn if you have to. I won't tell on you. But make sure you follow me, unless you think that critter can run faster than a .44-40 slug!"

The thoroughbreds had the limbs and the blood for long-distance speed over short-cropped prairie sod. Longarm admired Ruby's choice of horseflesh even more now that he saw they were polite, saddle-broken critters as well. It felt good to open up aboard a mount bred so tall and fast. Nothing felt as fast under a rider as a poor, dumb thoroughbred. The only reason nobody rode them for working stock was that speed was all a thoroughbred was good for. They had been inbred to total obedient idiocy. But right now, that was just what Longarm wanted from their mounts, and he got it.

Behind him, Cavendish wailed, "Not so fast! I ain't *used* to riding this fast, damn it!" But when Longarm shouted back that hanging took some getting used to, too, the prisoner just hung on to the horn and didn't argue any more.

Longarm ran them a good five miles and neither thoroughbred showed any signs of fatigue. But he knew that was because they were just too stupid to let a rider know when they were having a heart attack. So he reined to a walk and told Cavendish, "Sun's coming up. But we're out of sight from town, now. So we'd best rest these poor dumb brutes, some."

"My ass as well as my neck thanks you," Cavendish

said. "Where the hell have we been going all this time, Longarm? Unless I'm turned around, we're heading south. Ain't Denver west?"

Longarm said, "It is. We'd never make it that far on any horses. We're going to Kanorado and the railroad. It's only a twelve-hour ride, for more usual horses. These thoroughbreds ought to get us there in about six or eight. By now the trains should be running regular again and there's a westbound passenger train we can catch long before anyone from Coldwater can get there."

"What if they have someone waiting for us there?"

"They can't. Ain't no telegraph office in Coldwater. I generally thinks ahead, some, before I bust anybody out of jail."

Cavendish said, "I'd heard you were good. Could you take these cuffs off me, now? I ain't armed and there's no place I can run for, out here in the middle of nowheres much."

Longarm shook his head. "I never busted you out of there to make friends with you, Cavendish. I hardly ever treat a murderer more considerate than I have to."

"Damn it, I told you it was self-defense! It was him or me, Longarm! You'd have done the same thing in my place, I'll bet."

"You'd lose your bet, old son. Even if I bought your story about Pronto Malone issuing an invite to a showdown, which I don't, what you done was still premeditated murder. Self-defense is when a man has no other choice but to kill or be killed. You had a choice, according to your own words. You could have just rid out, like Pronto suggested."

Cavendish protested, "That'd have proved me a coward, damn it!"

"What do you call coming up behind a man with a double-barreled shotgun? Heroic? No, it won't wash, Monty. If you hadn't been pulling both triggers, even as Pronto turned, he'd have hit the ground with his hand on his gun at least. That's why they called him Pronto."

"You wasn't there. You just don't understand how it was."

"Save your bullshit about the code of the West for the grand jury. Let's talk about other dumb things you done, like lighting out on a stolen mount."

Cavendish whimpered, "Now that's a lie, pure and simple, Longarm! I've never stole a horse in my life. I told you I *bought* the damn fool brute fair and square. The rascal as sold it to me must have stolen it, see?"

"Well, that makes more sense than you riding it home, knowing it was stole. Who'd you buy it off? I'd best put his name on the wire lest he continue his dangerous hobby in other parts of these United States."

Cavendish shrugged and said, "Hell, I wasn't interested in his name. He said the horse's name was Pansy and I needed a horse."

"Which you got cheap, without pesky questions about no bill of sale. What did this horse trader *look* like, then?"

"He was just an old boy, Longarm, dressed cow but sort of shabby, like a saddle tramp down on his luck. He was around thirty, I reckon, with a nondescript face under a beat-up hat, creased Wyoming. He was sort of tall, now that I thinks back. About as tall as you, only built heavier. Wore a denim jacket and jeans, faded light."

Longarm drew a mental picture, grimaced, and muttered, "In other words, he looked like nine out of ten hands working any stockyard west of the Atlantic Ocean. Thanks a lot, Cavendish. With such a fine description he can't get any farther than the North Pole. Let's run some more. Sun's coming up."

* * *

133

As they saw the rooftops of Kanorado ahead, later in the day, no dust hung above the horizon behind them yet, so Longarm reined the lathered thoroughbreds to a walk again and told his prisoner, "Well, we made it. Westbound train's due in about an hour and a half, so there's no sense killing these poor brutes after all."

Cavendish said, "I hear a train whistle *now*."

Longarm replied in a disgusted tone, "That's the eastbound, coming *from* the west. Can't you see smoke when it's hanging high in the sky, you idjet?"

Cavendish squinted into the afternoon sunshine until he made out the distant plume of locomotive smoke. "Oh, yeah, I see her now. She's sure coming fast. Do she stop here at Kanorado?"

"Not unless someone aboard pays to get off here. That's the Kansas City Flier. We wants the Rock Island Denver Express, going the other way. They told me at the Kanorado depot she'll stop for a flag. Let's go see if they told me true."

They walked their mounts toward the rail line as the train from the west beat them to town, easy, and then stopped, to Longarm's mild surprise. It had discharged its local passenger or passengers and gone on by the time they rode across the tracks and reined in by the corral near the depot.

Longarm dismounted first, helped his prisoner down, and took out his handcuff key again, explaining, "I got a mess of chores to tend before our train pulls in and I wouldn't want you getting lost in the big city. So I'd best cuff your right wrist to my left. It won't show much, if you stick close."

Cavendish said he knew the form as he'd been arrested a time or two before, albeit usually on lesser charges. As Longarm cuffed their wrists together the corral hostler came over, looking sort of wary. Longarm said, "This gent's the prisoner. I ain't. I'm leaving these two thoroughbreds with you to be picked up by someone from the Last Chance, up Coldwater way. As you can see, I has my hands full. So I'll just bet you six bits you can't carry our harness and saddles over to yon depot, pard."

The hostler said Longarm was wrong and added, "You go on over and talk to the stationmaster about flagging the train if you like. I got time to pack your gear in two trips."

Longarm headed for the depot with Cavendish cuffed to him. They never made it.

"Have you gone loco?" Longarm grunted as Cavendish gasped, "Oh, no!" and tried to bolt for parts unknown. Since he was still cuffed to the bigger Longarm, his attempts to run resulted in the both of them revolving about a common center of gravity, like kids playing ring-around-the-rosy, while Longarm tried to keep his balance and warn Cavendish at the same time, "I'll whip your ass if you don't stop that!"

Cavendish just spun Longarm faster, gibbering with terror, and then, as guns commenced going off from both sides of them, Longarm realized what had spooked Cavendish and went for his own gun. The excited prisoner spun him backwards some more, walked into a bullet, and staggered back the other way as he went down, dragging Longarm with him as yet another round whizzed through the space Longarm had just been twirling through.

By the time Longarm landed flat on his back in the dust he had his own .44 out. It was awkward as hell shooting from that position, but he pegged a round at the nearest standing target and, to his considerable surprise, saw the gent spin around on one foot like a ballet dancer and join him in the dust, moaning, "You got me, Longarm!"

Longarm saw that the gent's own gun had fallen far from

135

him, so he rolled over atop Cavendish to see who'd been shooting at them from the other side.

A she-male form in a dusty red velvet dress lay face down at the foot of the depot steps with her high-button shoes hooked over the top step. Her gun lay even farther from her dusty blond head and she wasn't moving at all. He grimaced and unlocked himself from Cavendish, felt the side of his prisoner's neck, and muttered, "Shit." Then he got up, dusting off his pants with his Stetson, to move over to the wounded man who'd been throwing so much lead just now.

The hostler was ducked down behind a watering trough and nobody else had seen fit to join the party yet. Longarm and the wounded gunslick had the center of the street to themselves for the moment. Longarm kicked the fallen sixgun farther away and said, "Howdy, Tex. You heard about the run-in I had with your brother, huh?"

Tex Richardson glared up at him with hate-filled eyes. "I did, and I'd have dropped you in the same place you dropped him, had not that woman in the red dress gone loco just now! You never got me, Longarm. Does it make you proud, having a bitty blond she-male as your backup, you bastard?"

Longarm holstered his own unfired gun and hunkered down. "She wasn't trying to help me, Tex. She was trying to gun me, too. But you know what they say about too many cooks spoiling the broth. Where did she hit you, old son?"

"Don't touch me, you son of a bitch! My elbow's busted and I took one in the ribs as well. But I ain't kilt and we ain't settled, so I don't mean to owe you, hear?"

Longarm rolled him over onto his other side anyway, nodded, and said, "Same bullet shattered your elbow and bounced into your rib cage, where it still is. You're right,

136

Tex. You ain't shot mortal. Doc should have you patched up in no time."

Tex snarled, "And when he does, *watch out,* Longarm! For next time you can't hope to be so lucky!"

Duke Watson, the Kanorado law, came to join them, slow and thoughtful. He stared soberly at the three forms spread across the ground for his perusal and said wearily, "I figured nobody else would have been making so much noise, Longarm. What have we got here, the last act of Hamlet?"

Longarm got up. "Ain't sure, yet. Watch this mean one while I have me a look-see."

He walked past the cadaver of Montjoy Cavendish, dropped to one knee by the gal trailing down the steps of the depot, and rolled her over. She was a pretty little blonde, or had been, before she'd stopped a slug with her left eye. Longarm shook his head sadly and murmured, "I done you a *favor* by gunning that no-good gambler you was hooked up with, ma'am. I'm sure sorry you didn't see it that way."

Then he closed her one good eye, pocketed her little Harrington & Richardson .32, and went back to where Duke Watson stood over Tex Richardson. He saw the other lawman had already picked up the Texan's bigger sixgun and that some townees were approaching gingerly. Longarm told the Kanorado law, "What we has here is a case of murder or manslaughter, depending on whether Tex, here, shot that lady in the head intentional or not. Since she was hit spang in the eye at the tolerable range you can see for yourself, I'd have to say he was aiming pretty good at her in broad daylight."

The wounded man on the ground wailed, "Hold on, damn it! I wasn't shooting at no she-male, Longarm, I was shooting at *you,* you son of a bitch!"

"So you may say, Tex. But if you'll just look a little

137

closer, you'll see I wasn't the one you shot. You gunned a lady and an unarmed man. What makes you Richardson boys so mean, anyway?"

A short, portly man in a business suit joined them, asking Duke Watson what in hell was going on. Duke said, "We're still trying to sort it out, Your Honor. This here's Deputy U. S. Marshal Custis Long. The gent rolling about in the dust down there's a Texican named Richardson. Don't know who in the hell them dead folks might be. Seen the gal around town a couple of times. Dead man, there, is a stranger to me."

The small-town big shot turned to Longarm and said, "My name is Trevor and I'm the mayor, coroner, and justice of the peace here as well as postmaster. I'd like to hear your tale, Deputy."

Longarm had been working on a good one as he considered how to pluck the silver lining from this unexpected mess of clouds. He nodded. "The dead gent was a federal prisoner and, since he's dead, he don't concern you boys. But like Duke, here, says, the dead lady was a resident of Kanorado, shot in the head by this visitor to your fair city from Texas. So I'd say whether he hangs or not would be up to *you*, Your Honor."

He could already see the German band parading in the old rascal's eyes as Trevor said, "That's what we'd best do with the son of a bitch, then, for murdering she-males ain't lawful in this town."

Tex Richardson tried to sit up as he protested, "She was only an innocent bystander, damn it! I wasn't fighting *her!* I was fighting *Longarm*, there!"

Duke Watson kicked him flat and told him to shut up.

His honor sniffed and said, "Duke, you'd best get your prisoner a doc as soon as he's booked and locked up law-some. It'd be a shame to let him die from some infection before we can arrange for his proper hanging."

The man at their feet protested loudly, "You can't hang me up here! I'm a citizen of *Texas,* damn your eyes!"

His honor smiled down at him and purred, "Do tell? Well, it so happens I rode for the *North,* you poor murderous bastard! But that ain't why we'll be hanging you. We'll be hanging you for shooting a woman in a town where such critters is already all too scarce!"

Longarm looked at his watch and asked if it was all right if he headed back to Denver now. Duke looked at Trevor and when the justice nodded, said, "Sure. We don't need you to help us hang this son of a bitch. But what about your dead prisoner, Longarm?"

Longarm stared morosely at the body of Montjoy Cavendish, shrugged, and said, "I'd be obliged if you could see fit to bury him alongside the gal and bill my office, Duke. Riding trains with dead folk on a hot day can get sort of unpleasant after a time."

Chapter 12

Longarm's train got into Denver that evening long after the federal building had closed for the night. So Longarm checked his gear in the baggage room at the Union Depot, dropped by the Western Union near at hand to see if anyone had anything for him, and then went over to the Arabian Delight steam baths to clean some of the Ogallala Trail off his hide. Then he put on the clean shirt and underwear he'd brought along, threw the rags he'd ruined on the job away, and, once more fit to face civilized society, strolled over to the Black Cat to see how civilized it was.

He'd just settled himself in a booth in the back when his boss, Marshal Billy Vail, grumped in to plunk his broader butt down across from him.

"Howdy, Billy," Longarm said. "What are you doing in this uncouth neighborhood so late at night?"

Vail said, "Looking for you, of course. Heard you was back in town and knowed it was too early to find you in your furnished digs on the wrong side of Cherry Creek. I'm waiting to hear your story, Longarm."

Longarm reached in his coat for the report he'd scribbled aboard the train, leaving out some of the dirty parts, and handed it across the table to Vail as he asked, "Did Mandalian's crew catch up with the Rocking X?"

Vail nodded. "They did. Herding more Indian beef than the law allows. They said Reb Richardson and those two sidekicks of his you shot it out with in Kanorado did the shooting in the Osage Strip. But we still got the rascals on the stolen and rebranded Indian beef. So they'll be much older before they steals anyone *else's* cows! Get me a beer while I reads this latest fictional account of your pure-hearted quest for justice."

Longarm chuckled and carried his half-empty schooner to the bar to have it refilled and order another, without the needle, for his cleaner-living boss.

The barmaid, who knew Longarm of old, told him she was due to get off in an hour as she slid the drinks across the mahogany to him. Longarm smiled wisfully down the front of her low-cut dress as he replied, "Hold the thought, Miss Marcy. I sure hope I'm off duty soon, too. But that fat old rascal back there is my boss."

The strawberry blonde behind the bar said, "Well, you know where I resides, if you don't come too late, Custis."

He chuckled and carried the schooners back to the booth, recalling how late, as a matter of fact, he'd last come with Miss Marcy, who seldom got off before two or three in the morning.

As he sat down and slid Vail's drink to him, the bushy-eyebrowed marshal frowned across at him and said, "Well, it's done, but you surely did it sloppy, Longarm. I can see why you left Pronto Malone's killer to be buried by the Ogallala Trail. But, damn it, you should have brung Tex

Richardson back with you, shot up or not!"

Longarm looked innocent as he asked, "Whatever for, Billy? He was at their home spread in Texas when his brother gunned them boys in the Indian Nation, so we never could have convicted him on either the murder or cow-thieving charges."

"Just the same, he pegged shots at a federal deputy on duty for these United States, and that can't be constitutional, can it?"

Longarm swallowed some needled beer, belched, and said, "Since he missed me, how much time would a federal court have given him, boss?"

Vail grinned like a mean little kid. "Right. I'll forgive you for letting the local law hang him for gunning that gal who was out to gun you—unless, of course, he beats the charge."

"I don't see how," Longarm said. "He might have a shot at self-defense in a court run a mite more formal. But the judge as figures to try him on killing a local she-male citizen had dirty fingernails, rode for the North, and seemed mighty set on selling lots of tickets to the hanging."

Vail said, "Well, it's rough justice, but at least it's justice, in the end. For both the Richardson boys has been let off in the past, all too often, by jurymen who rode for the South."

He put the report away, saying he'd have Henry type it up in triplicate at the office in the morning. Then he said grudgingly, "You done right for a change, in your own rugged way. We can close the books on both the late Pronto Malone and the case he was working on. For once the cases was simple enough for you to solve without getting us into a war with Mexico or Canada and nobody who didn't deserve some hurting got hurt."

Longarm pulled out the wires he'd received from State-

142

line. "You'd better read these first, Billy," he told his boss.

Vail did so. The he shot Longarm a puzzled look and said, "So there's a few loose ends. There's always a few loose ends, old son. But what do they matter, since that asshole, Cavendish, won't be standing trial, now?"

Longarm said, "Montjoy Cavendish never killed Pronto Malone, Billy. He said he did. But that was to keep the town of Coldwater from hanging him any minute for *another* crime he never committed. The slick bastard naturally knew that once he was safe in front of a fair-run federal judge and jury he'd be free to retract his confession and go scot free, grinning like a shit-eating dog. You see, save for his own words, I just didn't have him nailed down solid for murdering Pronto. The only witnesses to the crime either described nobody much or a killer as wouldn't fit Cavendish worth a damn. Cavendish didn't own a pair of raggedy denim jeans and his prissy little feet was spurred and booted high-heeled when they caught him riding that purloined horse."

Vail shrugged. "The old piano player could have been wrong about the feet he said he saw. Hell, he could have made the whole thing up just to make himself sound important."

Longarm nodded, but said, "I already thought of that. But if we say not even Windy saw the killer at all, it gets even harder to prove it was Montjoy Cavendish. He was in Stateside at the time, like he said, but so were a mess of other folk. And, as that one wire says, his story about Pronto calling him on a fair-haired gal they was both after just won't hold water. Nobody in Stateside can recall such a single woman in town at the time. But they do recall that Pronto Malone, for once, wasn't even messing with the local Mexican talent. That reminds me, how's Flynn?"

"He's due out of the hospital in a few days. Can't re-

143

member getting shot. But you got the bastards as shot him, so what the hell. What's Flynn getting shot have to do with Mex gals in Stateside?"

"Nothing. I just worry about my pards, is all. The point about Mex gals is that Pronto for once was walking the straight and narrow. He wasn't drinking and he wasn't messing with the women in Stateside. I reckon, knowing he was already in trouble with the department, he was taking the case serious, trying to build some character before he had to face the music on that counterfeiting gal's charge. So what we wind up with is a case of murder, still unsolved. For, if it wasn't Cavendish it had to be somebody else, right?"

Vail grimaced. "Jesus, to think I left the comforts of my wife and slippers to hear such dismal news! All right, if you're so smart, who *was* it killed Pronto Malone?"

Longarm sipped some more needled beer, shrugged, and said, "Don't know yet. If you'd pay attention to that other wire from the saloon in Stateline, you'd see there *was* a ragged-ass stranger in town that day, just like Montjoy Cavendish said. The con man probably told me the truth about buying the stolen horse off him. Most gents on the run likes to change mounts as often as they can. Nobody recalls the gent with ragged jeans and big feet riding out, or on what. But he must have, since he ain't there now. Add it up, Billy. One witness says a man in raggedy jeans and low-heeled boots gunned Pronto. A ragged-ass stranger sells Cavendish a stolen horse just before the killing, making the mysterious saddle tramp at least an outlaw of *some* damned kind, and then he leaves town, sudden, before the local law gets around to counting noses after the gunsmoke clears!"

Vail sighed. "God damn it, that *works!* You figure old Pronto recognized a wandering gent from his pictures on one or more wanted flyers, Longarm?"

Longarm said, "Don't know. Pronto can't tell us now. But there's still a hole in that notion, boss. Had Pronto recognized his killer first, the fight should have gone the other way."

"Yeah, Malone was mighty fast with his gun hand. Try her this way. What if the stranger recognized Pronto first, knew he was the law, and just started shooting, impulsive?"

Longarm sipped some more as he thought. "Possible, but that means the killer was good as hell," he said finally. "Pronto had to be facing him as he swung that shotgun from a more friendly position."

"Couldn't he have called Pronto and fired as he turned, the way that con man said he did?"

"It might have happened that way. I mean to ask the rascal as soon as I catch him."

Vail shook his head soberly and said, "There's no way in hell anyone can hope to do that *now*, old son. The son of a bitch is long gone. The only witness who could describe him better is dead. Have you any notion how many men could be wandering about this land of our'n in raggedy denims, period?"

"It gets worse if he's had time to change his duds. But he still gunned a U. S. deputy and I don't mean to let him get away with it."

Vail swore under his breath. "Forget it, damn it. You'd have as good a chance trying to track down the James boys or Billy the Kid. At least we know what those rascals *look* like!"

Longarm said, "There's other lawmen looking for *those* wants, and they ain't done anything for me to take so personal. I said I mean to solve the Malone case entire, and I mean it, Billy."

"Look, it sticks in my craw to have one of my men gunned, too," Vail said. "But be sensible, Longarm. You'd be searching for a shadow on a trail gone cold."

"He ain't over on the Ogallala Trail," Longarm said. "I looked. And the more I looked, the more convinced I got that there was more to the killing than a trail-town shooting. It was cold, premeditated murder for a reason. A damned good one. Let's talk some more about the trouble he was in here in Denver, Billy."

Vail grimaced and asked, "Do we have to? With Pronto dead, the counterfeiting case is dead too. I wired you the grand jury let her go. We've been watching her ever since and it's looking more and more by the day she was just a two-bit gal the real counterfeiters had passing for 'em. Since she got out of jail she's been passing her ass for pay over in Golden. They say she's pretty, but just a cheap trail-town whore. Besides, she was in jail at the time Pronto was gunned. She's been watched since she got out. Nobody's contacted her but the usual whorehouse customers."

Longarm said, "Be easy enough to contact a gal in a house of ill repute just by knocking on the door and acting horny. Who's to say what a whore and a so-called customer might or might not say to one another in the privacy of a crib upstairs?"

Vail snorted in disgust. "You read too many penny dreadfuls. What would be the point of secret whorehouse meetings? She didn't have counterfeiting plates on her when she got arrested. It'd be dumb as hell to hide 'em in a whorehouse crib. So what's left? Who'd she meet so sneaky, and why?"

Longarm said, "Don't know. I mean to ask her. So you'd better tell me some more about her."

Vail took out his notebook, handed it over open, and said, "Copy this down, if you're willing to run over to Golden on your own time. I got better things for you to do on *duty*, damn it."

Longarm got out his own notebook to write down the bare bones facts Vail had written in his cramped script. When he'd finished, he handed Vail's notes back, put his own away, and said, "It'll be Saturday morning any minute. I know I owe you half a day, but I want the whole weekend off anyway."

"You got it," Vail replied grudgingly. "I'll expect you in the office early Monday morning, though. All you figure to pick up in Golden is a dose of clap. She's working in a mighty low-class joint, even for a little cow town."

Longarm drained his schooner and asked, "Want another, boss? I ain't leaving for Golden just yet."

Vail left the last of his own beer standing on the table as he got up and said, *"I'm* leaving. For *home!"*

Nobody was trying to stop him, but Vail stared sharply down at Longarm and said, "All right, what are you holding out on me, damn it?"

Longarm stared back up at him innocently. Vail said, "Don't try to teach your elders, boy. I know you of old and you're on to something. You think that gal had Pronto murdered so's he couldn't testify agin her as one of the arresting officers."

Then Vail scowled thoughtfully, shook his head, and said, "No, that leaves us with *another* infernal loose end! Why in thunder would a man riding to execute a deputy U. S. marshal steal an infernal *horse* along the way? He stole said horse in Coldwater, too, instead of getting off the train at Kanorado like you, Pronto, and everyone else with any brains did. It won't work, Longarm. If your ragged-ass prairie drifter is the killer, as you say, he can't be in cahoots with the counterfeiting gal. Any members of her gang still at large would have left from Denver here, and...oh, hell, *you* figure it out. It's way past my bed-time!"

He stomped out, cursing under his breath, as Longarm chuckled fondly. Then he waited until it was Miss Marcy's bedtime and went home with her.

Chapter 13

Since the strawberry blonde was an old pal and not at all shy, she and Longarm got right to the dirty stuff without hemming or hawing. But though she was young and healthy, Miss Marcy begged for mercy less than a full hour after they'd started, so they stopped to share a smoke and get their second wind.

As they cuddled together in the barmaid's featherbed she giggled and said, "I can see, this time, you didn't have such good hunting out of town, darling. I love it when you treat me like you ain't had a woman for at least a year."

He blew smoke rings at the ruby glass lamp across the way and said, "Well, a lady as nice as you deserves common courtesy, Miss Marcy. I sure admire your whorehouse lamp. It makes everything in here look rosy red and dirty."

She pouted. "That ain't no whorehouse lamp. I'm just sort of artistical. But how come you know so much about the illumination of whorehouses, dear? You've told me more than once you never likes to pay."

He chuckled. "That's how come I've never had to pay you, I reckon. I know you ain't no whore, Miss Marcy. As to how I might have thought your lamp was naughty, sometimes duty sends me to places I'd never in this world go on my own."

He blew another ring at the red light and added, "By the way, you may be hearing, around the Black Cat, about me visiting such a place of ill repute over to Golden come morning. I'd best assure you here and now that I'll only be going there on business, for I'd never cheat on you with no professional fancy gal."

She snuggled closer, reassured. He'd only told her the simple truth. The widow woman up on Sherman Avenue never charged, either.

The strawberry blonde naturally had to ask him what he'd be doing in a cow-town cathouse in the near future. So he told her, leaving out the other gals, about the case he was working on. He knew that whatever old Marcy was, she wasn't a counterfeiter. She always gave him the real thing.

She listened with some interest until he got up to investigating further in Golden. Then she said, "Your boss is right, dear. I can tell you true no serious counterfeiting gal would ever be working as a low-down pay-for-play."

He patted her bare shoulder as he replied, "That's why I told you the tale, honey. I was hoping she-male intuition might plug up some holes in my he-male reconstruction of the crime. How come you say no real lady crook could sell herself for cow-town prices?"

She reached for his free hand and pulled it into her lap, saying, "I know you admire what I got here. You just now showed me. But suppose I *was* to put a price on it? How much would you be willing to pay?"

Longarm didn't answer.

She chuckled fondly. "That's what I thought you'd say. I'm romantic-natured, too. You know screwing is my favorite sport. But the notion of laying in a crib taking on a mess of sweaty strangers makes me want to puke."

He fondled her absently as he objected, "Some gals are less romantic by nature, Miss Marcy."

She put her hand on the back of his to push his fingers deeper as she replied, "Sure. But leaving out such matters as who likes who to do what with what, where, us gals come in two basic sizes, dumb and smart. Whores by nature are just plain *dumb*. I can's see a woman used to living by her wits peddling her ass for cow-town prices."

He didn't think it would be polite to mention Miss Ruby back in Coldwater or some other fancy gals he'd met with brains. But as he thought about the few such gals he'd had friendly dealing with, he recalled that, in point of fact, most smart or even warm-natured whores tended to reform as soon as they got the chance. He told the strawberry blonde in bed with him, "I can see why you'd rather pump suds than work laying down, honey. But suppose you'd been living by your wits less lawful, got in trouble, and needed another source of income mighty sudden. Ain't it even possible for an adventurous gal to consider a career of temporary shame? Justice and Treasury can't go on watching that whorehouse in Golden forever, you know."

Marcy shook her head on his bare shoulder and said, "Lots of gals consider selling themselves after a hard day's work for little pay. It's a man's world, and once a gal discovers she ain't likely to become a princess, or even an actress, it can occur to her that since menfolk control all the money, and go crazy at the sight of an ankle, every pretty gal in the world is packing negotiable securities betwixt her legs. Would you pet my securities a might faster, dear?"

He found it sort of inspiring to himself as well, but asked, "Ain't you saying a pretty counterfeiting gal *could* get sort of practical in a hurry?"

She spread her thighs wider and started moving her hips teasingly as she replied, "Not if she's as smart as you all think she is. I reckon you would have to spend that day in a hairdresser's, listening to us gals talking practical, to follow my drift. You see, Custis, lots of gals give up and settle for selling their bodies to the highest bidder. But the *smart* ones *marry* for money!"

"That's a mighty mean thing to say about respectable married women, Marcy."

She sniffed. "A lot you know. That's why I insists most whores are stupid as hell. Consider the labor involved for the fruits of said labor. A poor dumb whore spreads her tired limbs night after night to strangers who can beat her up, dose her up, or just bore the hell out of her. Meanwhile, the pretty gal who wed one gent with a tolerable income only has to give him some now and again, whether she enjoys it or not. So, in return for less screwing in a month than a whore has to put up with in one night, the respected housewife can expect a man to take care of her for the rest of her natural life."

Longarm said, "Now that's what I call getting *paid!*"

The strawberry blonde said, "Good. You don't have to go over to Golden in the morning after all, and I got the day off. Speaking of time off, dear, what say we try to get ourselves hot some more?"

"Hold the thought till I finish this smoke. I'm all yourn tonight, Miss Marcy, but I still better ride over to Golden for a look-see at the mysterious she-male."

"You bastard! Can't you pass up a chance at *any* woman? I'll be damned if I'll share you with a whorehouse pig!"

He laughed and held her closer as he assured her, "Honey,

you couldn't get me to mess with that other gal at gunpoint! The whole point of my investigation is that another deputy did, she complained about it to the department, and then she or some damned somebody had him murdered. I'll tell you true, I don't even mean to be *alone* with her, with or without my pants on. For she could pull the same trick on me and, if it got down to her word against mine—well, my boss has a sort of low opinion of my morals as it is."

Mollified, the strawberry blonde snuggled closer and started stroking faster as she said, "Well, as long as you only means to *question* her. How come your department's so mean to you deputies? I'd have thought they'd have never taken the word of a crook agin that other deputy she framed. How come they didn't, Custis?"

He started to say the department had had a low opinion of the late Pronto Malone's morals, too, but he didn't. He kissed her and said, "Lord bless you, Miss Marcy, I hadn't thought of that!"

"Good. Can we go on now?"

"Wait, I'm thinking with my whole brain right now and your sweet little pussy is distracting as hell. Pronto *could* have denied her charges entire and it would have been just her word against his. Such things happen all the time when a lawman's dumb enough to be alone with a she-male prisoner for more than two minutes. But old Pronto *admitted* getting in her britches."

"Wasn't that sort of dumb of him, Custis?"

"It was. But Pronto never had much sense when it come to she-males. Let's see, now . . . She said he forced himself on her and Pronto said it was the other way around. I reckon I'll go with Pronto's story. A gal willing to work in a whorehouse wouldn't take much forcing, but a man who'd been offered it willing by a handsome gal, who then turned around and ratted on him, could get so flusterpated he might not be thinking straight when he was called on the carpet. That works to a point. But there's still a missing piece to the puzzle."

"Can't we just screw if you have to go on muttering to yourself?"

"Hush up, sweetheart, I'm almost there."

"Almost there? You ain't even *in* me, damn it!"

"In a minute! Have you ever had a thought just out of reach, like a name on the tip of your tongue? Pronto Malone was a womanizing fool, but he was still a professional lawman, and it wasn't like the Silver Dollar would be closed when he got off duty that day. The gal had to have tempted him with something more than her *body!* That quick lay on the desk was just to seal the bargain they made. She offered him a *deal,* a good one. That's why he confessed to laying her to Billy Vail. He was mortal shocked and disappointed when he heard how she'd double-crossed him. Their deal was more serious than some playful screwing on a desk. So serious he never considered what he was saying when he told Vail something he meant innocent, like, Hell, I only laid her to pass the time while we was waiting to go to the courtroom."

Marcy didn't answer. Her mouth was too busy with his limp organ as Longarm went on talking, really to himself. "It works. She got Pronto to *agree* to something. Then, whether he did it or not, she changed her mind and used his slap-and-tickle to muddle hell out of an already weak case against her. Meanwhile, Vail sent Pronto off to the Ogallala Trail to put some distance between a wayward deputy and some mighty steamed-up officers of the court. But don't you see, honey? Pronto still *knew* something, so he had to be shut up. Now, what could he have known about that gal and her pals that he didn't want to tell Billy Vail, even to save his own neck? It had to be something profitable as hell. They'd have had no need to kill him if he didn't still have some sort of hold on them!"

Longarm tried to remember every case of corrupted lawmen he'd ever been involved in. But, in truth, it was hard to think about such matters with a strawberry blonde eating him alive as she wagged her sweet tail in his face. So he put the matter aside for the moment as he inspired her back with fingers and tongue until she got hot enough to whirl about and do a split on his rejuvenated shaft.

But he couldn't help wondering, as he enjoyed the way she bounced up and down on him, how in thunder he was going to seriously question a lady in a whorehouse without giving way to his own weak nature, if she was even half as pretty as this strawberry blonde.

Chapter 14

She was prettier. Longarm found out, the legally correct way, when he contacted the Treasury agents staked out in a rooming house across the street from the biggest cathouse in Golden.

Golden wasn't much of a town. It lay in the foothills of the Front Range, just a few hours' ride northwest of Denver, snuggled between Lookout Mountain and a lower but steeper brick-red butte called Castle Rock. It had once been more populated. Back in the Sixties Golden had been the territorial capital and Denver had just been the mining camp of Cherry Creek. But the gold strike that had given Golden its population as well as its name had petered out to a modest trickle, and though they still dug a little coal, clay, and even gold from the complicated geology of the Front Range, the town was now half deserted. Such business as there was catered mostly to surrounding produce farms and stockmen passing through as they drove their herds to the Denver market from the higher, greener pastures of the high country farther west. More than half of the stock was sheep. So a gal working as a trail-break whore in Golden couldn't afford to be as snooty as the gals in real cow towns.

The Treasury men watching the whorehouse showed Longarm the photos they'd taken through the lace curtains as they waited for the mysterious gal to leave the crib so they could shadow her. The one in charge said she didn't even go to church with the other whores of a Sunday as he handed Longarm the plates.

Longarm studied the pictures of a mighty handsome lady who'd forgotten to draw the shades as she primped in her chemise at a mirror that didn't show in the pictures taken through her open window. She looked something like the beautiful English actress, Ellen Terry, save for having a bigger chest. Longarm couldn't tell from the photo what color her hair really was, so he asked. One of the Treasury men chuckled and said, "Dark brown, all over. It was warm the other night and she wandered about over there with the lamp lit and every stitch but her stockings off. We figure she's sort of advertising her wares to passing sheepherders, cuss her handsome ass. This job surely plays hell with a man's feelings. I'll confess, if I didn't know better, I'd know her even better by now. They only charges a dollar over there, and she's tempting as hell!"

Longarm moved over to the window, peered through the shades without moving them, and asked, "Do you reckon she has you boys spotted?"

Another Treasury man said, "If she knows we're watching her window, she sure must be a born prick teaser! Like Mel says, she never pulls her blinds."

Longarm consulted his notebook to get her fancy name right before he said, "We know Miss Cynthia Thornhampton enjoys the power she holds over most of us poor he-male brutes. That's the point of my speculation. She got one lawman in trouble, tempting him with her considerable charms. You all know, of course, that should one of us take advantage of her said charms, he'd be out of the race as a disqualified stud?"

There was a round of wistful laughter before someone sighed and said, "We know it all too well, and it hurts like hell."

Longarm stared across into the small, empty white-walled crib or mayhaps bigger bedroom. "Don't see her there now," he remarked. "You sure she ain't gone out? Is there a back door to that cathouse?"

A Treasury man said, "There is. A couple of your men from Justice are watching it from an abandoned mining shack up the back slope. She's likely screwing someone in another room over there. She's yet to bring a customer to the one with the open window. We figure she sleeps there and screws in a less elegant crib we can't see from here."

Another agent said, "Saw a couple of gents go in just a while ago. Looked like mining men. Damn, it's enough to make a poor old boy jerk off, thinking of all that stuff across the street, just out of reach!"

Longarm asked if any of them had noticed a big, big-footed man in raggedy jeans paying a visit to the whorehouse that day or any other. "I got a reason for asking," he added.

A Treasury man snorted in disgust. "How would you like your men in denim, numerical or alphabetic? That's a hardscrabble cathouse in a hardscrabble town, Longarm!"

"Yeah, the description I have ain't worth much," Longarm admitted. "Oh-oh, I see movement over there."

The four other men in the room with him crowded around him at the window as Miss Cynthia Thornhampton appeared in view, with a towel draped over one arm and nothing else, not even her stockings, to conceal her naked charms.

Someone gasped. "Hot damn, will you look at them tits!"

Another, more sedately, observed, "She's either come from taking a bath or screwing a customer—mebbe both."

The suspect draped the damp towel over a chair by the window and sat in it, still exposed from the waist up as she proceeded to comb her hair with one hand, eyes closed and head thrown back, sort of dreamy. Her other hand was in her lap, just out of their line of sight. And as she started squirming in her seat and stopped combing to throw her head back further, one of the Treasury men marveled, "Jesus, could she be doing what it sure looks like she's doing?"

Another said, "That's silly. Who ever heard of a whore jerking off? Why the hell would she *have* to, for God's sake?"

"Hell, Mel, *I* don't know. Mebbe she wasn't satisfied with the customer she just laid."

"Mebbe she knows she's being watched," Longarm said. "I've never been a whore, neither, but I've conversed with more than one about their profession. So I know that even the few who enjoys sex try to keep from coming while on duty. Really getting hot can mess up a fancy gal's pace. She ain't paid to enjoy herself. She's paid to get it over with as soon as she can. Yeah, that bitch is teasing us, sure as hell. Nobody really jerks off for pure pleasure with even a friend watching. She's doing that to tempt us from the straight and narrow!"

She was doing a good job, too. Despite his distaste for her criminal record and chosen way of life, Cynthia was pretty as a picture, and built so good it was sheer cruelty. Longarm ignored the tingle in his pants and said, "Well, now that I know what she looks like—and I'll likely never forget the sight—I'd best go see what my own sidekicks have been jerking off over, on the far side. You boys don't have to show me the back door to this place again. Just go

159

on admiring the view from your window and I'll get back to you later."

He went downstairs, remounted the livery horse he'd tethered in the back yard, and rode due west, not looking back, until he'd cut between frame buildings to a hillside side street he could follow in a wide circle, hopefully out of sight of the whorehouse.

He couldn't ride all the way to the mining shack his fellow deputies from Justice were staked out in. He had to tether his mount to the legs of an old mine tipple and walk along a cinder hillside path, trying to look innocent, until he circled around to the rear of the abandoned shack and entered.

The two deputies inside were at their window, too, with field glasses. He said, "Howdy, Matt, Virge. What's going on down the slope?"

Matt said, "Screwing," and Virge handed Longarm his field glasses, saying, "See for yourself. Another day of this duty and we'll wind up permanently horny."

Longarm took the field glasses, moved to the window, and adjusted the focus as he trained them through the cheese-cloth drapery on the rear of the whorehouse. He had a clear view of a close-set row of second-story windows, all wide open and curtainless, allowing for a shocking view into the working cribs of the establishment. Only two were occupied at the moment, but they were occupied indeed. A couple were screwing bare-ass in one crib. In another a naked gal was down on her knees, giving a grinning old man with a pot belly a French lesson.

Longarm whistled softly. "Don't they never close the blinds down there?"

Virge said, "Not when it's as warm as today. We figure, since this shack is supposed to be abandoned, and there's nothing else up here, they've gotten used to carefree ventilation. They naturally pay off the local law, so even if some kid hunting rabbits on the hill should get the shock of his young life, who's to care?"

Longarm handed the field glasses back. "Not me. Both them gents is ugly as hell and the gals ain't much. Have you seen the pretty suspect doing anything as interesting in the cribs with a big gent about my height, only built huskier?"

Matt said, "We ain't seen her doing nothing with nobody, damn it. The Treasury boys has told us what a looker she is without her duds on, too. But her crib must not be in our line of sight. It's just as well, most likely. Old Virge is right about this job making a man horny."

Longarm said, "I don't see a back door down there, but someone could likely get in or out via a first-story window, right?"

Matt said, "Sure. But we ain't seen any eloping whores or overly shy customers going in or out that way. You'll notice the siding is white, so even at night, such sneaky goings-on would be noticeable."

"Who's got the night shift here, Matt?"

"Dawson and Smiley. They'd likely have mentioned it had they seen anything sneaky going on. But what are we discussing, Longarm? What's to stop folks from just using the front door, regular?"

Longarm shrugged and said, "Nothing, I reckon. Has anyone thought to ask the local law about recent strangers in town, walking about in raggedy jeans and big old army boots?"

Neither answered.

"Right, I'll do so, then," said Longarm. "I'll see you boys later at the Pronghorn. It's the only place in town as serves unwatered drinks and has clean rooms to let upstairs as well. Where would I find Dawson and Smiley right now, if I wanted to?"

Matt laughed and answered, "You just said there was only one decent place to stay in town, Longarm. *We've* been here before, too."

He nodded and left them to go on talking dirty as they watched the show down the slope. He eased back to where he'd left his mount and rode down the center of Golden. He checked into the Pronghorn and had them stable his mount before he hunted up the town constable, who said to call him Pop, since everyone else did.

As they sat across Pop's desk in his office, Longarm brought the older lawman up to date. Pop was smarter than he looked and had already heard about and considered the case. He accepted Longarm's offered cheroot graciously enough, but said, "You federal boys are wasting your time here in Golden, son. I've already tossed your suspect's room. The madam is an old pal of mine. The only incriminating evidence your counterfeiting gal turnt whore has amongst her possibles is a she-male hygiene kit as might not be legal in some states. Colorado don't care if a gal takes care of herself or not. Saves the taxpayers money when whores don't get knocked up, for you knows what whores' kids grows up to be. So it's a favor to future generations of lawmen to let the sluts screw safe."

Longarm nodded soberly and asked, "Is there any way I could talk to your friendly madam without pounding on her door? I got my reasons for not crowding the suspect too close before I makes an arrest."

Pop nodded. "Sure. I knows better than to hang about a whorehouse with my badge showing, too. Time I pawed through that gal's stuff without a search warrant, I was acting unofficial. The madam said she was with a sheepherder at the time. When do you want me to set up the meeting, and where?"

Longarm said, "I'm staying at the Pronghorn, Room 3-B. After sundown sounds more discreet."

They shook on it and Longarm rose, but said, "By the way, about that big cuss in the old army boots..."

"He ain't in Golden," Pop said. "I tolt you my old pal Billy Vail wired me about that. I ain't saying I know ever' single face in town, but I know most, and I looks twice at them I don't. Besides, your notion don't make sense, son. Why would any gal have to meet a hired killer or whatever here in town when there's miles and miles of nothing but miles and miles all around?"

Longarm told Pop he had a point and left, feeling mighty frustrated. He went back to the hotel saloon, entered the tap room for some cool refreshment, and met Deputy Smiley already drinking ahead of him.

Smiley wasn't called Smiley because he had a friendly face. It was his last name. Smiley was some sort of breed, but nobody ever asked which tribe. Smiley hadn't smiled in living memory and had a scowl so mean it could curdle milk in the cow as old Smiley just rode by.

The dark, hawk-faced deputy told him the whole case was a waste of time, too. Smiley said, "It ain't as if this is the only mystery in the department's history, you know. We got lots of folk to look for. Some with decent descriptions, too."

"How many of them are wanted for killing a federal agent?" Longarm asked, grim-faced.

Smiley shrugged. "All right. What say we just arrest the damned Thornhampton gal and slap her silly till she tells us what in hell might be going on?"

Longarm shook his head. "Pronto treated her a lot more friendly and she still used it to beat us out of a trial. You stay well clear of her, Smiley. That's an order."

Smiley picked up the bottle of Kentucky mash he was working on, straight, and poured himself another shot as he grumbled, "Waste of time, even if we was allowed to screw her. She ain't got neither plates nor queer on her now, and the only suspects we've seen anywhere near her has been horny old men and pimple-faced boys. 'Fess up, Longarm, ain't we just sniffing up a blind alley?"

Longarm said Vail had given him until Monday to sniff something better or give it up. Then, since Smiley was morose company even when he wasn't drinking, he went to eat supper, strolled about town a spell looking at strangers' feet, and went up to his hired room to watch the sun go down.

The whorehouse madam turned up just after sunset. He bowed to her gallantly and offered her a seat on the bed, which was the only furniture worth sitting on in the sparsely furnished room. He sat on the one bentwood chair as they admired one another. The madam was a nice-looking motherly type few would have taken for a whore. Since she had to be over fifty, she likely wasn't any more. He could see how she and Pop could be good pals. Had she been a few years younger he'd have been tempted himself.

Pop had told her what Longarm wanted to talk to her about, so the madam wasted few words on the weather. "I know nothing about Cynthia Thornhampton's past, sir," she told him. "Since she's been a . . . resident at my boarding house, she's had no private visitors. She's a dear, quiet girl who seldom goes out and spends most of her free time in her own room, minding her own business."

"How *is* business, by the way, ma'am?"

"Don't be sassy, young man. You know full well that when I'm talking to the law I runs a boarding house for young ladies, official. I can assure you nothing at all improper has been going on in my place."

"How do you know the man I'm after hasn't never visited Cynthia Thornhampton, pretending to be a customer, for instance?"

He could see she didn't play poker much, but he couldn't see just why her big blue eyes were going so opaque all of a sudden. She sniffed and said, "I know what the man you're after looks like. I know who gets into my establishment at any hour, day or night, no matter *what* he looks like! Most of our customers are regulars. No stranger ever goes upstairs with one of my young ladies before I've had a considerable conversation with him. So I can give you my word no man who could possibly be the one you're after has been in my place to visit anyone."

She looked like she meant that, but her eyes were scared and she seemed to be hiding something. Longarm said, "You say Miss Cynthia hardly ever goes out, ma'am. How often *does* she go out?"

The madam seemed flustered as she asked, "Did I say that? How silly of me. As a matter of fact, dear little Cynthia *never* goes out. She doesn't even go to church. She seems rather shy, considering."

"She seems mighty pretty, too. Surely she gets more than the going rates for such visitors as she entertains?"

Again the madam's eyes went blank as she said, "That's none of your business! *My* business is not a federal matter and, as I see you're starting to ask rude questions of a lady, I think I'd best just leave!"

He rose to usher her out, politely. When she'd left he went back downstairs. Smiley wasn't there. He'd likely gone up to the shack to stand his turn on watch. The daytime deputies hadn't come down yet. They were likely enjoying some interesting sights through the field glasses as the evening shift filled all the cribs at once.

He called the barkeep over and said, "I'll bet you a dollar you can't tell me where the local lovers' lane in Golden might be."

The barkeep pocketed the cartwheel with a grin. "You have a local gal you aim to take sparking?" he asked.

"Something like that. Abandoned mine shafts and deserted old houses ain't too romantical. But if this town's like most, there has to be a place the younger and wilder set uses as a lovers' lane."

The barkeep nodded. "Castle Rock."

Longarm frowned. "That big red butte on the edge of town? I didn't know anyone could get *up* it."

The barkeep said, "It ain't easy, but that's the beauty of old Castle Rock. There's only one way up, unless a gal's daddy hails from the Swiss Alps. You work around to the north side of the butte till you sees a footpath worn pretty good in the shortgrass. It looks like it's heading smack into a sheer cliff, but it ain't. You scrambles over the scree at the base of the butte and there's a twisty trail even a gal in skirts can follow to the big flat top if she really aims to spend some private time with someone her family don't approve of."

"How big a space are we talking about, up on top?"

"Lots. Castle Rock is bigger than it looks. It slopes gentle to the east for acres and gets soft and fluffy with grass as you gets away from the cliffs. There's room for discreet snaking in the grass for one and all. You won't find many up there tonight, though. Sunday night's the night home gals is allowed to stroll around the block, as they say, with their young gentlemen callers."

Longarm thanked him and left. Since the town was so small, it only took him a few minutes to walk east, find the north face of Castle Rock, and follow the footpath as directed until he came to a comfortable-looking boulder and sat down. He didn't light a smoke. He just let a million years go by as it got darker and darker. The moon was due up in a while. Not as soon as it would have been after sundown farther out on the prairie. Aside from the moon rising twenty minutes later every night, anyway, sundown came earlier here in the foothills. The looming bulk of Lookout Mountain, rising to the west, shaded Golden in what would have been just late afternoon anywhere else.

He took out a cheroot and chewed it cold. Another million years went by. Then the moon peeked over the rim of the world to the east and his surroundings brightened considerable. He spied a sagging busted up bobwire fence he hadn't noticed before and muttered, "Yeah, a gal would be a fool to risk her skirts before the moon rose."

He waited with the patience of a fisherman, or an Indian, until he saw a she-male figure moving along the path toward him. Cynthia Thornhampton didn't see him until he stood up and said soberly, "Evening, Miss Cindy. You're under arrest. So hold out your hands."

She didn't. She stepped closer, smiling as if puzzled in the moonlight, and laughed teasingly before she said, "Oh, I'll just bet you're one of those silly boys who've been watching me from across the street, right? You know you can't arrest me. But, all right, since you went to so much effort to get me alone, I can be a good sport."

She reached down to hoist her skirts and show him what a good sport she could be, not having anything under said skirts, as she added, "Could we go find someplace soft and comfy, honey?"

He reached out, took her by one hand, and said, "This'll do fine." Then he led her over to the old bobwire fence and cuffed her to a post. "You can drop your skirts now. The reason I'm patting you down like this ain't to be taken personal. Just want to see if you snuck out with a shooting iron."

She had. He removed the derringer from between her proud breasts and said, "Shame on you. Now listen to me, girl, and listen tight. You may think you can yell loud enough to be heard atop them cliffs, but as of now all I has on you is aiding and abetting. So unless you aim to grow old and gray at needlework in a federal pen, you'd best behave yourself, hear?"

She sobbed, "I don't know what you're talking about! All right, I'm a whore. Is that a federal offense, damn it?"

"No. But you ain't no whore, neither. You've been hiding out in a whorehouse, sure enough. But you've been paying, not getting paid. I'll figure out later how you've been sneaking out at night with my pards watching. But I knew you had been, as soon as your pal, the madam, worked so hard to convince me the other way. You just wait here, Miss Cindy. Me or your boyfriend will be down soon enough to rid you of that fence post, depending."

She was still protesting her innocence as Longarm found the trail up that the barkeep had told him about. It was steep as hell and in places one had to move on all fours. There was no way to crawl to the top without dislodging an occasional rock to go skittering down with considerable sound. So when a male voice called down, "That you, honey?" Longarm just kept going without answering. He'd made it almost to the top before his persistent admirer insisted, "Damn it, Cindy, is that you or ain't it?"

Longarm looked up, saw a figure looming against the stars above him, and drew his .44 as he replied, "No, Pronto, it ain't."

He might have said more had he been talking to anyone else. But when Pronto Malone slapped leather it was time to fire at him. So Longarm did, and it was still a near thing. Pronto's gun cleared leather and went off. But since he was hit in the chest his aim wasn't so good.

He just teetered back and forth on his wobbly legs, firing round after round down the cliff at nobody in particular as Longarm hunkered in a rock cleft and held his own fire, hoping the son of a bitch would fall the right way.

Pronto didn't. After emptying his gun down the side of Castle Rock he dove after it, and it seemed to take forever before he hit bottom with an awesome, wet thud.

Longarm sighed and moved on up to the top. As he reached it, he spotted a campfire in the middle distance and saw figures outlined against moon and fire, coming his way with guns.

He said, "Everybody freeze and grab some stars!"

Then, when nobody did, he opened up on them, aiming at the one with the twelve-gauge first. There were four of them and one of Longarm, but the tall deputy was hunkered low with the blackness of Lookout Mountain behind him, so the fight didn't turn out as one-sided as it might have, had not he had the sense to move each time he fired and gave his position away.

When it was over, Longarm reloaded and moved in for a closer look at the gang. One was still breathing. Longarm kicked him in the ribs to gain his undivided attention and said, "Let's see if I got it right. You boys has been camped up here in the sky, waiting for things at ground level to cool off, while the gal smuggled food and water up to you from her whorehouse cover. You didn't have to worry about local lovebirds telling on you once you chased 'em back down the butte, gentle. For what kid's about to tell his folks he was up atop Castle Rock with a gal?"

The lung-shot owlhoot died without saying anything.

There were no horses up here, of course, but Longarm

was going through their possibles around the fire when he heard a familiar voice cry out, "Longarm? Is that you doing all the shooting up here?"

Longarm called back, "Over here by the fire, Smiley. I wasn't doing all the shooting. I had me some help."

The morose-looking breed joined him as Longarm removed a flat package from a bag and said, "Kick them coals up for me, will you, Smiley? I need some light on the subject I just found."

Smiley kicked the fire higher. Longarm grinned and said, "Yep. There are counterfeiting plates, sure as hell. It's starting to make sense at last. The gal knew she was being watched. But we had no idea what her confederates looked like. Didn't know, until just now, who one particular confederate *was*, neither."

Smiley growled, "Would you just stop talking to your fool self and tell me what in hell is going on? We heard shots and come running to find one gent spattered like jam on the rocks below and a gal handcuffed to a fence."

"That was my doing. I trust somebody's guarding her?"

"What for? She's dead. Somebody parted her hair with a .44 slug. Was that your doing, Longarm?"

Longarm grimaced and said, "The gent I sent over the cliff was pissing lead at everything down there before he went, so I reckon we just got lucky."

Smiley gazed about. "You call this *luck?* There ain't one goddamn suspect left to question, Longarm!"

"Don't matter. We've recovered the plates. The gang's out of business. So minor details don't hardly matter now."

"You know who that was as shot the gal and then tried to dive on top of her, Longarm?"

Longarm didn't answer. It was wrong to lie to a fellow lawman.

170

Chapter 15

Now that he'd figured most of the razzle-dazzle out, Longarm had to keep it going despite the fact that the gunfight
atop Castle Rock had drawn every lawman and just about
everyone else in town to the scene. The curious townees
weren't the problem. The other lawmen were. It was only
natural for any lawman to crow some when he solved a
tough case and Longarm knew what his own first impulse
had been when the key piece to the puzzle identified itself
with a familiar voice.

Getting the bodies down off Castle Rock before they got
stiff kept everybody busy for a spell. They tended to agree
with Longarm that old Smiley's suggestion that they just
roll the bastards over the edge of the cliff seemed a mite
untidy.

Once all six cadavers were neatly lined on the walk in
front of the town hall for everyone to admire until they
could be salted down and shipped to the Denver morgue,

it transpired all five of the dead men had proper, albeit likely fake, I.D. None of them were dressed in raggedy denim and one, of course, had no face worth mention. The dead gal's I.D. was no problem, of course, even though a couple of townee gals fainted when they saw her face. Longarm suggested and Pop agreed it might be best to cover her face with a kerchief.

Longarm and the other lawmen went inside to talk in private. When Longarm produced the counterfeiting plates and handed them over to the Treasury men, the boss of their crew held them up to the light and marveled, "Hot damn! I know who made these! Hardly anyone in the business engraves on steel plates by hand, and those who do so are seldom this good. These plates was engraved by old Hamp Thornhill in Baltimore. He used to work for the Washington mint, legal, but he went bad when he retired and seemed discontented with his modest government pension. Jesus, ain't that pretty engraving? That gal out on the walk never would have been caught passing them twenties had the paper been better. She was dumb to try and pass queer printed on regular bond paper in that Denver bank. Bank tellers snap paper bills all day long, and when the paper don't snap right . . ."

One of his fellow agents asked, "Ain't old Hamp Thornhill *dead,* Mel?"

The crew chief shrugged. "He is. But so what? Anyone can see the gang outside inherited these plates he made. Wait a minute, they say Hamp Thornhill had a family. His old woman died some time back. But, yeah, he left a son and a daughter behind."

Longarm said, "There you go, Mel. I can't tell you which of them dead gents outside might be the old counterfeiter's son, but the gal we was watching called herself Thornhampton. Add it up."

Mel nodded, saying, "That explains why they couldn't just run off on her with the plates, knowing we was watching her. She was more than a queer passer, she was *kin*. Aside from being the sister of one of the gang, she was likely married up or at least mighty sweet on at least one other member of the gang. We know now, thanks to your interview with the madam, that she was neither a shy virgin nor a real whore."

One of Longarm's own crew, damn his eyes, said, "We're still missing something here, gents. That camp atop Castle Rock was risky as well as temporary. So why in hell didn't the gal just run off with them all in the dark? I can think of a dozen ways she could have done so and, once in the mountains just to the west..."

Longarm said, "You'd best check that out, Matt. Run over to the whorehouse and interview the madam some more about secret exits. Don't pistol-whip her if it can be avoided."

As Matt headed for the door, his sidekick, Virge, said, "I suspicion *I* know why they was lurking about. They was *waiting* for somebody."

Longarm said, "You better go with Matt and make sure he don't get in trouble with them fancy gals, Virge." Virge grinned and ran out after Matt.

It almost worked. Neither Smiley nor his night-shift sidekick were deep thinkers. But one of the Treasury men said, "That might be a good point to follow up on, gents. We still haven't accounted for that ragged stranger who gunned Pronto Malone. I'll bet they sent him over to the Ogallala Trail to kill Malone after agreeing to wait for him here in Golden. What say we stake out Castle Rock and see if the rascal shows up?"

Mel looked disgusted. "Sure. Hardly anyone in town knows Longarm, here, just found the hideout and shot it up."

Longarm suggested, "Is there any natural law saying a man can't change his duds, Mel? For all we know, the ragged stranger is laying on the walk outside, dressed neater."

Mel was too smart. "Could be," he said, "but in that case you arrived on the scene just in time. For if the killer had rejoined them, they had no reason to tarry in such a risky place, and the gal was on her way to meet them tonight, remember?"

Longarm nodded and told him he was smart as hell. But the Treasury man wasn't through showing off his savvy. He frowned and said, "The one thing about this case that don't make a lick of sense is their *motive* for gunning that deputy of yourn, so far away he should have been out of sight and mind. Have you any notions on that, Longarm?"

Longarm shrugged and tried to look dumb. That worked, for hardly anyone ever suspected a man of admitting he was stupid unless he really was.

Another Treasury man said, "It's my feeling Pronto Malone must have *knowed* something. He was alone with the gal long enough to lay her on a desk. Who's to say what she might or might not have let slip in the heat of passion?"

Longarm brightened. "There you go. That would explain why she turned on poor old Malone after she cooled down and got to thinking clear again."

Mel frowned and asked, "In that case, why didn't Malone come forward with such new evidence as he uncovered in his delicate questioning of his prisoner?"

Longarm said, "He might not have known he had it. Gals say all sorts of things when they're going at it hot and heavy and, most of the time, as you must all recall, us gents ain't really listening."

The head Treasury agent nodded thoughtfully and said, "That works. She offered herself willing, like Malone said.

He was a horny fool and we know she was horny, too. When she cooled down, she recalled she might have been indiscreet with her mouth as well as her body. So she ratted on Malone to get him out on the street where he could be gunned. Only he was sent over to the Ogallala Trail instead and—yeah, like I said, it works. Works good enough to put her in my report that way, anyway. We'll never know what the slip-up might have been now, but as the gang's out of business, what the hell."

Another Treasury man objected, "But what about the ragged killer?"

Mel frowned at him and said, "He's going down in my official report as one of them five dead gents outside, whether he is or ain't. What do you want, egg in your beer? We got *other* cases to work on, you know, and with the plates recovered, the son of a bitch is out of the counterfeiting business, dead or alive." He turned to Longarm. "You can still hunt for him if you want. This case is closed, as far as *Treasury* knows or cares."

Longarm said that sounded fair, so they shook and parted friendly. Outside, as he, Smiley, and the other federal deputy headed for the telegraph office to wire in their own version, Matt and Virge caught up with them.

Matt said, "Well, the gal was slipping in and out via a side door and the empty house next door, with neither team able to cover that angle, God damn it to hell."

Longarm smiled and asked, "How come you're so displeased, Matt? It ain't your fault the gal was so sneaky. We knew she had to be working it some damned way. I'd never have met her at the base of Castle Rock if she'd been screwing some sheepherder in the house."

"The madam explained everything, scared skinny and batting her big blue eyes at us," Matt said. "She confessed the counterfeiting gal was only a boarder there, like you suspicioned, and confessed further that she'd been slipping out the side way with food, water, and even dirty books for her pals atop the butte to read. And then, sweet Jesus, she said we could have all the comforts of her establishment, from booze to broads, free, if only we would put in a good word for her with the judge!"

Longarm laughed. "Well, none of us has to be at the Denver office before Monday morning, and I see no need to arrest the old bawd now. So I fail to see how you could be compromising yourselves as the arresting officers if you took her up on her offer. Of course, it's up to you boys whether you tell her you ain't arresting her or not, for a spell."

Matt and Virge exchanged glances. Virge asked Longarm if he really meant that and, when Longarm just grinned, the two of them ran off like redbone hounds who'd just sniffed some mighty interesting game.

Smiley scowled and asked, "How come you're suddenly so free and easy with department rules, Longarm? You fuss at me every time I gets a little drunk, damn it!"

Longarm stopped in front of the Western Union, propped a foot up on the steps, and said, "If they ain't arresting anyone they're on their own time. You'll be free to get drunk as a skunk or join them in that cathouse once you get them cadavers on their way to Denver for me. So what are you following me about for?"

Smiley nudged his sidekick and they went off together, grinning slick. Longarm felt pretty slick, too. But he still had to work on old Billy Vail, and the boss was cleaner-living than most of his deputies.

Monday morning, back in Denver, Longarm made a special effort to get to the office early for a change. Fortunately the widow woman on Sherman Avenue still had her noisy alarm clock, so he made it.

Vail had beaten him to the federal building, of course. The night watchman there had gotten so tired of opening up early for the marshal that they'd given him his own keys to the front door downstairs.

Longarm sat across the desk from Vail as the pudgy, shrewd old cuss went over his report along with a copy of the Treasury agent's report and some criminal records from the files. Vail took so long that Longarm had his cheroot smoked halfway down when his boss looked up at him and said, "All right. As usual, your field work was a mite untidy. But since no innocent women or children got gunned by you personal, I can find it in my heart to forgive you. All but one of the men you shot it out with in Golden the other night have been dug out of the yellow sheets. One was the brother of that gal, the old rogue engraver's daughter. The other three we have names on was known associates. But they was counterfeiters, not gunslicks, as they discovered to their cost when they tried to shoot it out with you. So the only one who might have been the killer we was after was the one who lost his damned face doing a swan dive off Castle Rock. His fake I.D. failed to jibe with anyone in the files, innocent or guilty. Your report here says he commenced the festivities by firing on you first. So, yeah, I'd say you nailed the killer of Pronto Malone."

Longarm sighed and said, "I sure hope you're in a jolly mood this morning, Billy. I worked hard on that final report, and to begin with, there ain't one actual word of perjury in it. But, since I have to tell the truth to *you*, damn the regulations, I'd best admit I left just a few things out."

Billy Vail scowled at him in a way that hardly indicated a jolly mood. But their relationship was based on mutual trust. Longarm said, "I'd best start at the beginning. It's

177

sort of a complicated tale and, to tell the truth, I'm just guessing at some of the fine print, albeit I can't see how else it would work."

"Will you cut the bullshit and get to the *point*, Longarm?"

Longarm took the cheroot from between his teeth, snubbed it in the copper ashtray on the desk between them, and said, "Once upon a time there was a slick old counterfeiter who died and left little more than a criminal record and a set of mighty good twenty-dollar silver certificate plates to his less skilled son and daughter."

"That's already in both reports, God damn it!"

"I still like to start at the beginning, Billy. The kids and their pals came west, since they was too well known in Baltimore to pass queer there on piss-poor paper. It was the paper that was their undoing. Nobody in the gang knew half as much as the old dead counterfeiter. They had to run off the queer on the best bond paper they could buy in a stationery store and hope for the best. As we know, it wasn't good enough. They passed some. Then the gal, Cindy, got caught at the Drover's Trust. The bank dicks held her for Treasury. Treasury locked her up to stand trial. Being said trial was to take place here in the federal building, Justice as usual provided a deputy U. S. marshal to escort her to and from court."

Vail called Longarm an awful name and said, "Tell me something I don't already know, damn your eyes! Pronto Malone was assigned to guard her, found himself alone with her too long to resist temptation, and they got to acting dirty, right?"

"Not exactly, Billy. They may or may not have made friends atop that desk down the hall, but that was just a side issue. Did you know old Pronto worked for a spell in a paper mill back East, right after the War?"

"Sure, now that I think about it. It's in his employment file."

"That's where *I* found out he'd once worked at making paper. He did lots of things after the War. But I reckon the six months he spent in that paper mill taught him more about making paper than that gal and her gang knew. I read a book one time that said a man can make his own paper with a skilled hand, a washtub of pulp, and a window screen. I'm sure Pronto knew Treasury bills are printed on paper made from a mixed pulp of linen, cotton, and silk. *I* do, and I ain't never even worked in a paper mill."

Vail looked puzzled instead of annoyed as he asked, "Are you suggesting our own Pronto Malone told that counterfeiting gal how to make the right kind of paper, Longarm?"

Longarm shook his head. "Ain't *suggesting*. *Saying*. He likely just twitted her about it some at first. You know how he liked to brag. It was likely the gal's own notion to proposition him. If she heisted her skirts, it was just to seal the bargain. She heisted her skirts easy in the presence of the law, as I recall."

"What bargain are we speaking of, Longarm?"

"To turn rogue, of course. Pronto was a half-ass deputy who'd been passed over for promotion more than once, and none of us are paid what we're really worth. You'd had him on the carpet more than once for messing up. He knew his job wasn't too secure and, had he been happily married, he'd have fooled around less on his pretty little wife. So add it up. An insecure deputy facing middle age with no decent job and a wife he no longer cared for. The counterfeiting gal, on the other hand, was offering a glamorous and profitable criminal career as well as her not-bad body. I got to see her naked, too, and I can tell you a horny skirt chaser like old Pronto would have jerked off, wistful, for

179

the rest of his life, had he turned such nice stuff down."

Vail grimaced and said, "Said life didn't last too long, once I sent him over to check up on the Richardson brothers."

"Don't get ahead of the story and mix us up," Longarm said. "As I put the deal together, they agreed to get her off so's he could run off with her and her gang for travel and adventure. Pronto was no good, but he knew his law. So, to get her off, he let her file a complaint against him and then he owned up to it like a poor, dumb fool. So it *did* get her off."

"That works. I was wondering why he admitted laying her when it was his word agin a knowed criminal's. And to think I tried to help him by sending him out of town till the dust settled!"

Longarm smiled crookedly and said, "It's a good thing you're so soft-hearted, for it screwed them up fearsome. He had to go where you sent him, lest you get even *more* upset and suspicious. So he contacted her outside confederates and arranged to meet up with the gang later, once she got out. Then he went over to the Ogallala Trail and acted the good little boy. He really checked brands, laid off the redeye, and didn't even mess with the willing local gals. So he was bright-eyed and bushy-tailed when opportunity come knocking on his door."

"What opportunity was that, Longarm?"

"Got to go back to another once upon a time, when a saddle tramp drifting down the trail stole a horse in Coldwater and kept going till he got to Stateline."

"Oh, you already told me about the drifter selling the stolen horse to that poor idiot, Montjoy Cavendish, in Stateside."

"That was only a confusing side issue, Billy. Once he'd sold the horse, the horse thief had nothing to worry about

180

as well as the cash Cavendish laid on him for the brute. So he hung about Stateside, dismounted, till he could mayhaps steal another horse. In his relaxed state, he met up with Pronto Malone."

"And killed poor Pronto with a shotgun!" Vail cut in.

Longarm shook his head and said, "I sure wish you'd let me tell it, Billy. The saddle tramp never gunned Malone. It was the other way around. Don't ask dumb questions about whether they looked more or less like one another, for had they not, it wouldn't have seemed such a golden opportunity to Pronto. Suffice it to say, Pronto noticed they was about the same size and build. I can think of a dozen ways Pronto could have got the shabby saddle tramp to change clothes with him. Knowing what a bully Pronto was, I'd guess he just got the horse thief alone, threw down on him, and made him do so. Then he frog-marched him around to the front of the saloon and blew his face off, cold-blooded, before lighting out of town. One witness caught a glimpse of the low-heeled boots us deputies all wear, but that was all and, in the confusion, nobody thought to ask what might have happened to a dead deputy's *horse*. I did, last night. Stateside wired back that nobody there has any notion where the horse he'd stabled behind the hotel was. Until they got my wire, they hadn't studied on it."

Across the desk, Vail was staring at him as if he'd just opened a box of snakes between them.

Longarm nodded. "He naturally changed his duds as soon as he was clear. Then headed back to meet up with his sweetheart and her pals to start a new life from scratch. He circled a lot to cover his tracks. So he'd just about got there when I made it to Golen and inquired some about local lovers' lanes. I knew they wouldn't be holed up in anything as dumb as an old mine shaft or an empty house, with the town crawling with lawmen. It's a good thing I arrived when I did. The gal was fixing to make her break and, as others have said, once the gang was up in the high country they'd have been free to start up again in other parts."

Vail shook his head as if to clear it and said, "Longarm, that is about the wildest tale I've ever heard, and I once arrested Soapy Smith. Do you have one lick of *proof* to all these wild allegations about a fellow deputy?"

Longarm shrugged. "Not now. Old Pronto landed on his face right after I recognized his voice atop Castle Rock. Up till then, I was only guessing. But it had occurred to me that when you just can't find any sign of a murderer, the murder might not have taken place. Fortunately, neither the Pronto I sent over the cliff nor the Pronto we buried decent on the edge of town a mite earlier could be identified for certain by a loving mother now. I noticed, when I shot old Four Eyes, that getting shot in the face tends to distort one's features a mite, and that was only with a .44-40. Shotguns and diving off cliffs do a better job. So, like I put in that report, the mystery guest to my shootout atop Castle Rock will just have to be buried under the name he gave in his new, fake I.D."

Vail scowled and said, "The hell you say! I know you'd never try to sell me such a crazy story if it wasn't *true!* The son of a bitch *rogued* on me! If there's one thing I hates worse than a rogue lawman, don't tell me what it is, for I might have a stroke just cussing it so hard! Pronto Malone was a purple-pissing disgrace to the Justice Department and I mean to have his *ass* for it!"

"Now don't get your bowels in an uproar, Billy. I detested the rascal so much myself that I shot him. But there's nothing you can do to hurt him further, even if we dig him up."

Vail gasped and said, "That's right! We buried him at the taxpayers' expense, in a fine bronze casket!"

"No, we never. We buried another man entire, and I doubt like hell anyone else would have any use for that casket now. It might be best to let dead dogs lay, boss."

Vail thought before he said grudgingly, "All right. We won't dig up a stinky horse thief. The real Pronto Malone gets buried in potter's field now. For he's no deputy of mine, once I put things to right in the records!"

Longarm nodded soberly and said, "You do that, boss. No sense in that pretty little widow woman Pronto left getting a government pension she can't be entitled to now."

It worked. Billy Vail simmered down, stared soberly back at him, and asked, "Does anybody else know the full details of this case?"

Longarm shook his head. "Nary a soul but you and me, Billy. That's why I worded my report so delicate. I figured it was up to you to decide about anything I might have left out."

Vail nodded grimly and said, "You figured right. It hardly seems fair, but the son of a bitch was mean enough to his poor woman whilst he was alive. Don't seem right to let him hurt her further, from the grave."

He picked up his pen to initial and approve Longarm's report as written. Then he said, "I reckon someone ought to go and tell Mrs. Dotty Malone the murder of her husband has been avenged. I know for a fact, for my own woman told me, that old Dotty wasn't at all sorry to bury the son of a bitch—or whoever she buried. But it's more fitting she should hear the news from her late husband's department rather than reading about it in the *Post*."

Longarm yawned and said, "I'll ride out to her house and tell her if you like, Billy."

But Vail scowled. "No, you won't. You're on duty today, and I know all too well how you feels a widow woman should be consoled, you rascal! I'll go tell her myself, prim and proper. When you get off duty this evening, late, you can just go console that widow woman of yourn up to Sherman Avenue, hear?"

Longarm reached for another cheroot without answering. It was none of Billy Vail's business that it was another gal entire's turn to be consoled tonight.

Watch for

LONGARM ON THE ARKANSAS DIVIDE

seventy-first novel in the bold
LONGARM series from Jove

coming in November!